Banjo Tully

Justin D'Ath lives in Queenscliff, Victoria. He has written 50+ books for children and young adults. His *Extreme Adventure* series has sold half a million copies and been made into a popular TV series. Justin has twice been short-listed in the Victorian Premier's Awards, has written six CBCA Notable Books and gained numerous Yabba/Koala nominations.

http://www.justindath.com/

Also by Justin D'Ath

Pool

Three

47 Degrees

BANJO TULLY

Justin D'Ath

For Margaret, Queen of op shoppers

First published by Ford Street Publishing, Melbourne,
Victoria, Australia

2 4 6 8 10 9 7 5 3 1

This publication is copyright. Apart from any use
as permitted under the Copyright Act 1968, no part
may be reproduced by any process without prior written
permission from the publisher. Requests and enquiries
concerning reproduction should be addressed to
Ford Street Publishing Pty Ltd,
162 Hoddle Street, Abbotsford, Vic 3067, Australia

Ford Street website: www.fordstreetpublishing.com

First published 2021

Title: Banjo Tully / 2021

Text copyright © Justin D'Ath 2021

Cover design Sabine Hopfer

Target audience Upper Primary/Lower Secondary
ISBN: 9781925804904 (paperback)

 A catalogue record for this book is available from the National Library of Australia

Printed in Australia by McPherson's Printing Group

1

Ride to School Day

You see more from a horse than you do from the school bus. But Banjo wonders if that's an advantage. Sweeping his gaze back and forth as Milly trots bumpily along the edge of the gravel road to town, all he sees is red dirt, empty dams and kilometre after kilometre of sagging fences that no longer keep anything in or out. At least on the bus there are other things to look at and think about. Or talk about, if someone sits next to you. But since the Lawsons sold their farm last October, no one sits next to Banjo. That's the problem when you live further from school than everyone else and yours is the first stop – you can't choose who to sit next to on the bus; it's those who get on after you who choose. Sometimes Banjo finds himself resenting Archie Lawson for moving away, even though he knows that isn't fair. Archie's parents didn't want to sell up and leave; the drought sent them broke. They live in town now, only three streets from school. Archie usually walks there, but today he'll be riding.

Riding his bicycle.

Banjo knows he's going to get into trouble. Ride to School Day means ride your bike, not your horse. It's about fitness and encouraging students to get more exercise. Really, it's aimed at townies (like Archie, now); people on farms get enough exercise just going about their daily lives.

Just *surviving*, which is a word Banjo's parents use more and more lately.

The distance from his house to the bus stop is 1.6 kilometres – he calculated it last year as part of a Year 8 Maths homework exercise. Every morning he rides there on his bike and locks it to the fence by the letterbox. But he's not allowed to bring it on the bus; he asked yesterday and Damian, the bus driver, said no.

Everybody who comes to school on their bike today is going to get a free movie pass, donated by the principal's brother, who runs the cinema. Banjo knows he won't get a movie pass – he'll probably get a detention notice. He doesn't care. Well, he *does* care, but he wants to make a point. It's only townies who can get free movie passes. How is that fair?

Banjo's phone starts ringing in his backpack, *Zzzz zzzz zzzz*. He's surprised – normally there's no mobile coverage this far from town. Perhaps it's because he's on a horse, not on the bus. It'll just be someone from school, Archie or Tamati or Usman. Whatever they're calling about can wait until he gets there. Banjo can't afford to stop and talk, he doesn't want to be late. If he and Milly arrive after the bell, nobody will be outside to witness his Ride to School protest.

He'll get in trouble for nothing.

Banjo's parents have no idea what he's doing. They would never allow it. He had to plan things carefully. His mother left for work at six as usual, so he wasn't worried about her. But his father chose today of all days to rehang one of the gates in the sheep yards, which would give him a clear line of sight all the way down the 1.6 kilometre drive. To avoid being seen, Banjo had to saddle Milly behind the tractor shed, then ride her in a big loop around the wheat block to the gate near the Lawsons' old boundary. It added about two kilometres to the journey, plus three extra gates to open and close – not a good start. Still, they left home before seven, so Banjo is reasonably confident they'll get to school on time.

He brushes a fly away from the corner of his eye. That's another thing you don't have to put up with on the bus. The fly resettles in the exact same place; or it might be a different fly – about a million of them are swirling around Banjo's head. Around Milly's head, too. They target eyes, ears, lips and nostrils, anywhere they might find moisture. Everything around here is thirsty – including Banjo, who forgot to bring water.

Water should have been the first thing he thought of.

A vehicle is coming, a four-wheel drive towing a

horse trailer. It drags a red cloud of dust behind it. Banjo slows Milly to a walk and edges her off the narrow road to make room. The approaching vehicle slows, too. It's a shiny silver Land Rover. Banjo waves, but he doesn't see who's inside or if they wave back. His phone is ringing again. He ignores it. With a nudge of his left leg, he steers Milly back out onto the road. Then he double-clucks his tongue, loosens the reins and she breaks into an easy canter.

Milly is a good horse, intuitive and rider-friendly. Banjo has known her all his life. He's been riding her since he was eight years old. Now they are both fifteen. But in horse years, Milly is closer to Nan Tully's age. It was Nan who taught Banjo to ride. The big bay mare belonged to her before she became Banjo's. Nan and Milly used to compete in showjumping events all over the state until Nan got too old. When she and Pop retired and moved to the coast, they left the family farm for Banjo's parents to run. Milly stayed behind and became a stock horse. Now all the cattle are gone and Milly doesn't have much work to do. Like Nan and Pop, the old mare has earned her retirement. Even so, she seems to be enjoying today's workout. Banjo reaches forward and pats Milly's neck, making a silent promise to ride her more regularly from now on. Only not so far next time, he decides. And certainly not to school.

They are almost there. The gravel road surface gives way to bitumen and they pass the big sign saying: *Welcome to Big River, Level 4 Water Restrictions Now In Place.*

A little white dog yaps at them from someone's dusty front yard; perhaps it doesn't see horses very often. Are horses even *allowed* in town?

Not for the first time this morning, Banjo questions the wisdom of what he's doing. It isn't going to prove anything. And who really cares about a free movie pass? But deep down, he knows it isn't about movie passes at all, it's about something bigger. Banjo can't put it into words. It has something to do with his parents being forced to sell all their cattle because there was nothing for them to eat. And his mother going back to work six days a week so the *family* could eat. And all those dry, dusty paddocks with nothing in them. None of which is something anyone can change, but together they are important.

People should know about them.

Banjo isn't late. Still half a block from school, he sees a line of twenty or thirty cars waiting their turn in the kiss-and-drop zone. So not everybody has ridden to school. There are quite a few bikes though, many more than you see on a normal day. The lollipop lady struts to the centre of the road and blows her whistle, allowing a procession of dismounted riders to cross. Others weave along both footpaths and hop off when they reach the walking zone. Banjo is still too far away to recognise anyone, but judging from the size of them compared to the lollipop lady, most of the kids with bicycles are Year 7s, 8s and 9s. The senior students, the 10s, 11s and 12s, probably consider it uncool to turn up at school on a bike. Banjo wonders if he will be like that next year. He hopes not. Anyway, he won't get the opportunity, will he? Unless his parents lose their farm like Archie's did, which is not totally impossible.

'Nice horse!' someone calls.

Banjo turns and sees a group of four girls watching him. They are inside the school fence, sitting on one of the benches outside the library. He recognises them – they are all in Year 10 – but he doesn't know their names. The tall red-haired one was in the *River News* when she broke the state record for the high jump.

'Thanks!' he yells.

'What's his name?' asks the small girl with black hair sitting next to the high jumper.

'Milly,' Banjo tells her. He rides up onto the footpath and stops at the fence. 'It's a she, not a he.'

The girl makes a wry face. 'Sorry. I don't know much about horses. She's very big. What are you doing?'

'Coming to school.'

'On a horse?'

'It's Ride to School Day.'

All four girls laugh. The one talking to him stands up and comes over to the fence. She takes a step back when Milly swings her big head around.

'You do know it's about bikes?' she says.

Her friends laugh again. They are making fun of him. Banjo doesn't blame them. It's pretty stupid what he's doing. But it's too late now – he has arrived at school on his horse and he has to go through with it.

'I'm protesting,' he announces. 'I live twenty-one kilometres from town. That's too far on a bike.'

'You've ridden *twenty-one kilometres*?' asks the girl at the fence.

'A bit further, actually – we had to make a detour.'

She looks puzzled. 'So . . . isn't there a bus?'

'If I came on the bus, I wouldn't be riding to school,' he explains. 'You have to ride to get a free movie pass.'

It sounds really lame when he says it out loud. Banjo's face feels hot. He'll have to do better when he faces his next audience, which might even include the principal, Mr Gunston. He nudges Milly's ribs and she begins clip-clopping along the footpath towards the school gate.

The girl keeps pace with them on the other side of the fence. 'You must really love movies.'

'It's not about movies,' Banjo says, 'it's about what's fair.' He wishes he could explain it better, but his thoughts are scrambled. Half his brain is planning what to say when he reaches the gate.

If he could travel back two hours in time, Banjo knows he would do the sensible thing and catch the bus.

'Well, good luck with your protest, boy from Snowy

River,' says the friendly Year 10 girl, giving him a little wave as she turns back to rejoin her friends.

Banjo knows she's referring to that old movie about a guy on a horse (who's a man, not a boy). She's making fun of him.

But boys can be heroes too.

2

Mad Dingo

Ms Cartwright, who teaches PE and Health and Lifestyle, stands just inside the students' entry gate with her iPad. One by one, those with bicycles file past her, pausing while she records their names.

'Well done, Daisy,' she says to a little Year 7 whose adult-sized retro bike is nearly as tall as she is. 'And you are in . . . ?'

'7L,' says Daisy.

'Thank you.' Ms Cartwright scrolls and taps, then looks up to see who's next. 'Good morning, Archie Lawson. 9B, isn't it?' Scroll, tap. 'That helmet should be on your head, not on the handlebars.'

'I took it off when I got to the walk zone, Ms C.'

'Surely it would be easier to wear it,' the teacher comments, but Archie has already moved on. 'Next!'

The girl next in line hasn't come forward, she's staring back over her shoulder. Those behind her are looking back, too. Ms Cartwright follows the general gaze and spots Banjo and Milly at the rear of the line. The teacher is peering directly into the morning sun. Using the iPad to shade her eyes, she steps out onto the footpath. 'Who's that?'

'Banjo Tully,' he says. '9B.'

'You can't bring a horse to school.'

Banjo feels foolish. This was such a bad idea. 'But it's Ride to School Day.'

He expects Ms Cartwright's response will be much the same as the Year 10 girl's – *You do know it's about bikes?* – but, instead, she comes marching down the footpath and squints up at him. 'Is this your idea of a joke, Banjo?'

'No,' he says weakly. He wonders if he should dismount. He hears someone calling out in the background, 'Tully, you mad dingo!' Not helpful, Archie.

'It's just . . .' Banjo's mind has gone blank. Everything he planned to say has deserted him. 'I live too far away to come on a bike.'

He says nothing about the movie passes – that just seems stupid now.

The teacher glares up at him. 'Well, you can turn around and ride straight back home. Frankly, Banjo, you're the last person I'd expect to pull a ridiculous stunt like this.'

She used to be his pack leader in Scouts, but now that he's moved up to Venturers, he only sees her at school. He has to be careful not to call her by her Scout name, Raksha. 'Sorry, Ms Cartwright.'

Three Year 7 boys pushing BMXs squeeze past on the street side of Milly. As soon as the footpath is clear, Banjo pulls gently on the right rein to turn her around.

'Where do you think you're going?' asks Ms Cartwright.

'You told me to go home.'

'Well, I've changed my mind.' She makes a shooing motion with her iPad at the waiting cyclists. 'You lot go to your classes – the bell's about to ring.'

'But you haven't got our names yet,' says one of the BMX boys.

Ms Cartwright takes a deep breath. 'Listen up, everybody!' she calls. 'Here's what's going to happen: I'll be in my office for the first half of recess; go there as soon as you're out of class and I'll get your names then.'

The cyclists file slowly into the school grounds. Soon it's just Banjo and Ms Cartwright. She says, 'You live out past the old saleyards, don't you?'

'Other direction.' He points. 'We're at the very end of Drover's Road.'

'That's quite a distance.' Ms Cartwright strokes Milly's nose. Unlike the Year 10 girl, she seems at ease with the big mare. 'I assume your parents don't know about this, Banjo?'

'No. They don't.'

'They'll have to be told.'

He shrugs. His father has probably already noticed that Milly is missing. He'll see Banjo's bicycle still in the tractor shed and put two and two together.

'They'll have to come and collect your horse,' Ms Cartwright says, 'or arrange for someone else to collect it.'

'Can't I just ride her home again?' asks Banjo.

The bell rings and Ms Cartwright waits for it to stop. She shakes her head. 'You're at school now, Banjo. You're our responsibility until classes finish this afternoon. Someone will have to come for your horse.'

Banjo wets his lips. His father will go ballistic if he has to bring the horse trailer all the way to town to get Milly. He says, 'I can ride her home *after* school, Ms Cartwright. It would save everyone a lot of trouble.'

She looks him in the eye. They both know that the only person in trouble is him. 'Don't push your luck, Banjo. I've already told you twice that you are not riding home.' She brushes away a fly. 'Wait here, I'll go and talk to Mr Gunston.'

Two mothers push identical strollers up the footpath towards them. When they see the horse and rider outside the high school gate, they cross to the other side of the road.

'You're in the way here, Banjo,' growls Ms Cartwright, who just *told* him to wait here. 'Take your horse around to the staff car park. There's a small patch of lawn – well, it used to be lawn – on the left as you go in. Wait for me there.'

While Ms Cartwright goes to see the principal, Banjo rides Milly along the front of the school and turns right onto River Bend Road. The staff car park is 50 metres ahead, just past the gym. The sound of the second bell clangs across the empty basketball courts. Everyone will be bustling into their classrooms. 9B starts Friday with a Maths double, but after that they have Industrial Technology, which is probably Banjo's favourite subject, then there's Japanese with Mr Nakamura and that's always fun.

And today school finishes early because of the holidays. Two long weeks at home. It was better before Nan and Pop moved away. And now Archie's gone, too.

Milly's hooves play a slow drumbeat on the footpath. Here's the gate. The reins dangle loose in Banjo's hands and his legs stay relaxed. There's a voice in his head – it's an echo of what Archie yelled earlier: *Tully, you mad dingo!*

Banjo checks in both directions for traffic, then he steers Milly out onto River Bend Road and urges her into a trot.

3

Survivors

River Bend Park, where the Aboriginal Studies teacher, Mr Hayes, takes the new Year 7s to visit the Canoe Tree every year, is a 15-minute walk from school. But it's only five minutes on a horse. When Banjo's class came here two years ago, Archie got three demerits for frisbeeing Usman's hat into the water. That would not have happened today – the river is so low that nobody would be able to throw a hat that far. There's a joke going around that they're going to change the town's name from Big River to Empty River.

Banjo dismounts and lets his helmet clatter onto the iron-hard ground that used to be a grassy picnic area. He drops his backpack beside it. The drinking fountain hasn't been used for ages; the bowl part is dull with dust and holds a collection of dead leaves and dried gumnuts. Banjo hopes it's still connected. Wiping the nozzle clean with his thumb, he presses the button. Yay! The water spurts out warm at first, but Banjo doesn't wait for it to run cold. Water is precious. And it tastes good, regardless of temperature. He keeps drinking until long after the flow has become cool. He didn't realise how thirsty he was.

Milly snorts and tosses her head. She's watching him drink.

'Sorry Mills, your turn next,' Banjo promises, wiping his chin. Removing her saddle, he drapes it over the back of a chipped old park bench angled towards the empty river. Then he grabs her dangling reins. 'Come with me,' he says.

He leads Milly around the fenced-off Canoe Tree, then down past a faded sign that used to say *No Dogs, No Camping, No Swimming*. Some doofus has used a marker pen to change the bottom line to *No Water*. There *is* water, though – a telltale line of reeds wiggles its way along the middle of the wide, red-brown riverbed. The rest is bare clay, baked into a mosaic of randomly shaped tiles that wobble under Banjo's school shoes. It's bizarre to think that big fish used to swim where he and Milly are walking now. When Banjo's dad was a boy, he and Pop caught a giant cod at River Bend Park that weighed 44 kilos. Now there's just a trickle, barely enough for tadpoles.

Banjo removes Milly's bit and bridle so she can drink. She's just as thirsty as he was. He feels guilty for riding her all this way. But she seemed to enjoy it. Life must be pretty boring for her now that Nan's gone and there's no longer any cattle work for her to do back on the farm. She must get lonely, too. He makes a silent promise to pay her more attention from now on. It's school holidays now, so they can go riding every day. Officially, the holidays don't start until 2:30 this afternoon, but, for Banjo, they have begun already.

He wonders what's happening back at school. He pictures Ms Cartwright bringing Mr Gunston out to the staff carpark, only to discover that the prankster who rode a horse to school has shot through.

I told him to wait for me here! she'll growl.

The principal will be angry too. He's walked all this way for nothing. *What's this boy's name again, Tara?*

Banjo Tully, Ms Cartwright will say. *He's in 9B.*

Mr Gunston will wheel around and go striding back towards Admin. He's massively overweight, his face will be shiny and red. *Leave this to me, Tara*, he'll puff. *I'll give his parents a call.*

At least Banjo won't have to face Mr Gunston until after the holidays. In two weeks none of this will seem so bad. The principal might even have forgotten about it, but Banjo can't avoid his parents for two weeks.

'I'm in so much trouble!' he says.

At the sound of his voice, the big mare raises her head. She stares at him, water dripping from her black, velvety muzzle. Then she swings away and begins feeding on the lush, green grass that grows all through the reeds lining the water's edge. Who wouldn't be hungry after hoofing it for 21 kilometres?

he thinks. And that's just the half of it. There are still 21 kilometres to go. No way will Banjo make his father drive all the way to town with the horse trailer. He rode to school, he'll ride home again. But there's no hurry.

'Take your time, Mills,' he tells his grazing horse. 'We've got all day.'

It will be better to wait until late in the afternoon, when it's cooler, before they go home. In the meantime, he'll have to let his parents know what's going on. Mr Gunston will have phoned them by now; they'll be worried. A short text message to his mother should do the trick.

Banjo feels sorry for his parents. They have so much going on in their lives right now. Although they are careful not to talk about it in front of him, Banjo knows the money situation is getting tight. They seem worried all the time. Will they lose their farm like Archie's parents?

He hates this drought.

Banjo swipes at a fly. There are lots here. They buzz around his head and they're all over Milly, too. They have settled in their hundreds on her sweaty brown coat where the saddle was – it looks like she's been rolling in cinders. Every few seconds, she flicks an ear, or blinks when one crawls in her eye, but mostly she ignores them. Flies are just something you learn to live with here. The drought doesn't seem to have affected their numbers. They're survivors.

'Like us,' Banjo says, thinking of his parents.

River Bend Park is roughly one kilometre from the edge of town. Nobody would visit on a weekday. Why would they visit at all, Banjo asks himself, now that there's no river? It's a good place for him and Milly to spend the day. There's water, there's shade under the Canoe Tree, there's somewhere a horse can graze and Banjo has his school lunch for later. There's a morning snack in his lunchbox, too – three Anzac biscuits from the batch his mother baked last weekend. Even though recess won't be for another hour or so yet, Banjo is hungry already.

And he's not *at* school, he's on holiday – he can eat whenever he likes!

Milly won't run off. He leaves her fossicking about among the reeds and walks back up to the picnic area to get his Anzac biscuits.

His phone is ringing again when he arrives, *Zzzz zzzz zzzz*. It won't be Usman or Archie this time, Banjo thinks as he fumbles his backpack open. They're in Maths, lucky them, ha ha! It'll be one of his parents. He's too slow to answer, but the screen tells him it was his mother. There are two earlier missed calls as well, both from 'Home'. That's the landline – there's no mobile service on the farm. His father has left a voice message.

Banjo hesitates. He's a bit scared to hear what his father's going to say, but he steels himself and dials 101.

'Banjo, where in the blazes are you?' his father asks. 'You need to bring Milly home right now! Honestly, you have put me in a really awkward position. They are here. They have driven all the way up from Gippsland. Call me back.'

Yikes! thinks Banjo. Dad isn't happy. But what's he talking about? Who's driven from Gippsland? Banjo isn't even sure where Gippsland *is*. He listens for a moment longer, but the recording has finished. *Ping!* goes his phone, telling him there's a new voice message. This one is from his mother – she must have called while he was listening to his father's message.

'Darling, I know you must be upset about Milly. Your father and I should have told you. Please call me. I've explained it all to Mr Gunston and you aren't in trouble at school . . . Oh, and you aren't in trouble with Dad and me either, darling. Just call us.'

Puzzled, Banjo replays both messages. Neither of them makes a whole lot of sense. Some people have arrived from Gippsland and he's supposed to know who they are. And his mother thinks he's upset about Milly, for some reason. What's going on?

Banjo turns and looks down into the wide, brown riverbed. There's Milly. She's okay. The phone feels warm against his sweaty palm. What is it that his parents haven't told him?

He finds his lunchbox and carries both it and his phone over to one of the graffitied picnic tables.

Sitting on the hard wooden seat, Banjo munches an Anzac biscuit and listens to both messages for a third time. None of it makes sense. He eats another biscuit, then stands up and walks across to the drinking fountain to wash down the crumbs. He knows he's stalling. But he doesn't want to talk to anyone yet, especially his parents. He needs to work this out. Something is going on, something to do with Milly that they haven't told him.

That's when Banjo remembers the silver Land Rover with the horse trailer that passed him, going in the other direction, on his way to school. *They've driven all the way up from Gippsland.*

He calls his mother and she answers immediately. 'Darling, where are you?' she asks.

Banjo ignores the question and asks one of his own.

'Are you and Dad selling Milly?'

4

The Canoe Tree

His mother hesitates before replying. The silence only lasts for a couple of seconds, but that's long enough to confirm Banjo's suspicions.

His parents are selling Milly!

'I thought you knew,' she says softly.

'No.'

'Didn't Dad say anything?'

'No.'

'Oh . . .' She sounds confused. 'Well . . . why did you run away with her this morning?'

From where he's standing, Banjo can see Milly moving slowly along the bed of the river, her head down among the reeds. Don't *you* run away, he thinks. 'Because it's Ride to School Day. Didn't you talk to Mr Gunston?'

'He phoned me,' says his mother. 'But I'm pretty sure he didn't mention that. Isn't it for bicycles?'

Banjo rolls his eyes. He didn't call his mother just to have that conversation all over again. 'You can't sell Milly, Mum. She's mine.'

There's another pause. This one lasts longer than the first. His mother must be feeling really bad. *She deserves to*, he thinks.

'Milly doesn't actually belong to you, darling,' she says finally. 'She's part of the farm.'

'No, she isn't,' Banjo counters. 'Nan gave her to me. The day before she and Pop left, she said Milly was mine now.'

His mother is silent.

'Ring her, Mum, if you don't believe me.'

'Of course I believe you,' she says quietly. 'But your father and I didn't know. Honestly, darling, we didn't think you would mind. You hardly ride her anymore.'

Banjo catches the school bus at 7:15 each morning and doesn't get home till nearly 5 pm. That doesn't leave much time for horse riding. 'The holidays start next week,' he tells his mother. 'I was going to ride her every day.'

'I'm really sorry you had to find out about it like this,' she says. 'But in all honesty, darling, we didn't have much choice but to sell her. It costs so much to feed a horse these days. And she's going to a good home. The people who bought her own a riding school down in Gippsland – she'll get lots of exercise and have other horses for company.'

Banjo has been watching Milly while he and his mother talk. The mare is calmly grazing down in the riverbed. 'I can pay for her food,' he says. 'I'll get a holiday job at McDonald's.'

He hears his mother sigh. 'It's too late, darling. Her new owners have driven all this way to collect her. We can't simply tell them the deal is off. I'm really . . .'

Their conversation is interrupted by the crunch of tyres on gravel. A big white ute with a 1,000 litre water tank on its tray has just driven in through the gate from River Bend Road.

'Gotta go, Mum,' says Banjo, ending the call.

The logo on the side of the ute reads *Big River City Council*. It pulls up near the bench where Banjo left Milly's saddle and a small, dark-haired man climbs out. He studies the saddle for a moment, then stares down into the riverbed where Milly is feeding. Finally, he looks at Banjo.

'Is that your horse?'

Banjo nods, even though he's not sure if Milly really *is* his anymore.

The councilman swats at a fly. He's wearing a name badge: *Tuan Le*. 'It probably shouldn't be here,' he says.

Banjo shrugs. 'She's not doing any harm.'

'Here's the problem,' says Tuan Le, who's trying to look stern but is not quite succeeding. 'The council has just appointed a new Council Bylaws Officer and from all reports he's a bit of a stickler for the rules. He comes by here quite often, even on weekends.'

'What's a Council Bylaws Officer?' Banjo asks.

'They used to be called dog catchers,' explains Tuan.

Banjo has heard about the new dog catcher. Usman's labradoodle puppy got nabbed by him a couple of weeks ago and they had to pay a $100 fine to get it back. Usman said the guy looked like Jabba the Hutt.

'It doesn't say horses,' Banjo argues, pointing at the *No Dogs* sign.

'I don't think *any* animals are allowed here,' Tuan says thoughtfully. Then, unexpectedly, his face lights up in a grin. 'Except kangaroos.'

Banjo doesn't grin back. Wordlessly, he fetches Milly's headgear from the bench and walks down into the dry riverbed. Nothing is going right for him today.

Milly lifts her head as he approaches and allows him to fit the bridle. She's a good horse. Banjo still can't believe his parents have sold her.

They had no right!

When he and Milly arrive back at the picnic area, Tuan is attaching a thin, green hose to a small pump connected to the water tank on the back of his ute. He gives Banjo a wink. 'I'm not really supposed to be doing this – don't tell anyone.'

Banjo has no idea what he's talking about, so he simply nods noncommittally and gets to work re-saddling Milly. Meanwhile, Tuan unspools the hose and drags the free end over to the Canoe Tree. Passing it beneath the wooden fence, he lets it flop down onto the dust and dead leaves near the trunk.

'No school today?' he asks casually on his way

back to the ute. Of course he has noticed Banjo's high school uniform, but it's none of his business whether Banjo is at school or not.

'I decided to have the day off.'

'Well, it's a great day for it,' Tuan observes, even though almost every day has been like this – fine, sunny, dry – for as long as Banjo can remember. Tuan pulls on the starter rope and the pump burbles to life. A twitch runs along the hose, like a snake waking up, then a dark stain begins spreading slowly across the parched ground beneath the huge, old river gum.

Tuan comes and stands beside Banjo. Despite their slightly awkward conversation about school, the councilman seems perfectly at ease. He points up into the tree. 'Notice how much sky you can see.'

Banjo follows his gaze. He can see lots of blue sky through the mostly-bare branches. A pair of crows fly over, high up, calling back and forth to each other, *cawww, cawww, cawww.*

'A few years ago,' Tuan says, 'you could stand here and you wouldn't see any sky at all.'

Banjo can't remember how much sky was visible through the Canoe Tree's branches when he came here in Year 7. They only looked at the trunk.

Tuan stoops and gathers up a handful of fallen gum leaves. 'They drop their leaves like this to conserve moisture,' he explains. 'This tree has been doing it for the past eighteen months or so. It's a sign of stress.'

'But it won't die?' Banjo says, half statement,

half question. It's a gumtree, after all – they grow in deserts.

'Who can say?' Tuan closes his fingers around the leaves, making a crackling sound. 'All I know is it needs water. So I sneak down here every Friday and give it a drink.'

Banjo remembers Tuan's earlier remark about not telling anyone. He asks, 'Why do you have to sneak down?'

'Strictly speaking, I'm only supposed to do the council gardens,' Tuan confides. 'Which is fair enough, I guess, given the water situation. But this old guy deserves VIP treatment.'

'We learned about it in Aboriginal Studies,' volunteers Banjo. Mr Hayes explained how his ancestors, who he called the Paakantji mob, prised off a big slab of bark about 300 years ago to make a canoe. You can still see the scar – a deep, surfboard-shaped depression in the tree's gnarly trunk. 'It's nearly 1,000 years old.'

Tuan nods. 'It must have got through many droughts in its time. But this could be the worst of the lot.'

Kneeling to tighten Milly's girth, Banjo surprises himself by saying, 'I absolutely hate it.'

'Hate what?' asks Tuan.

'The drought. It's wrecking everything!' To Banjo's horror, his eyes fill with tears. He wipes them with the back of his left wrist, carefully keeping his face turned away. 'We can't even afford to have a horse anymore.'

Tuan is silent for a moment. '*This* horse?' he asks finally.

'Yes. My parents sold her without telling me.'

'That's tough.'

'They reckon she belongs to the farm, not to me,' Banjo continues. He can't believe he's telling this to a stranger, but he seems unable to stop himself. 'Nan – my grandmother – gave Milly to me when she and Pop retired and moved to the coast a couple of years ago. But she didn't tell my parents. And now they've sold her without telling me.'

Tuan gazes into the distance. 'Is it very far away, your farm?'

'Twenty-one kilometres,' Banjo says.

'And you rode all the way here on your horse?'

Banjo straightens from tightening the girth. He can't be bothered explaining his silly Ride to School Day stunt all over again, so he gives the shortened version: 'We went to school first, but horses aren't allowed there.'

Over on the picnic table, his phone is ringing again. He walks over to see who's calling. It's his mother, which doesn't surprise him. He lets it ring out, then slips it into his backpack and threads his arms through the shoulder straps.

'Are you on your way home?' asks Tuan, watching Banjo clip on his helmet.

'Not straight away.' Banjo uses the bench as a mounting block to swing himself up into the saddle. 'Milly will need to rest up for a bit before we set out.'

Tuan pauses for a few moments, as if pondering something. 'Do your parents know you're not at school?'

'Yes. I was talking to Mum when you arrived.'

'That's okay, then.' Tuan points downriver. 'If you want somewhere quiet to spend an hour or two until you and your horse are ready to go home,' he says, 'there's a nice shady spot about a kilometre further on, where the old caravan park used to be.'

'Thanks,' Banjo says with a smile.

The friendly councilman's eyes twinkle. 'The dog catcher won't bother you there,' he adds.

5

Silly Milly

Banjo dismounts and strokes Milly's neck as he takes in his surroundings. He has never been to the caravan park before. He's gone past it lots of times, but it's not somewhere you visit if you live locally. Every summer and school holidays it became a mini town, crowded with caravans, cars, tents and bicycles. And people were everywhere. Now it's deserted.

Big River Caravan Park shut down last year. It was on *60 Minutes*. They did an entire show on the drought and how it affected everyone, not just farmers. They interviewed the caravan park's owners, Mr and Mrs Vigano. Banjo sort of knows them because their kids went to his old primary school. In the interview, Mr Vigano explained how people stopped taking holidays here after the river dried up. He said the caravan park had been a family-run business for 22 years. Mrs Vigano stood next to him while he was talking. The camera zoomed in for a close-up of her face – two fat tears made snail tracks down her cheeks.

Banjo wonders where the Viganos are now. He

hopes they're okay. The caravan park they used to own looks like it has been abandoned for longer than just one year. Leaves and fallen branches litter the roof of the little house-cum-reception office where they must have lived. One of the windows is broken. A single caravan remains in the far corner of the park – it leans sideways on the stub of a missing wheel and its door hangs open.

Tuan was right – nobody will bother Banjo and Milly here.

There's lots of shade, thanks to several big peppercorn trees scattered across the site. But finding water proves to be a problem – someone has removed the knobs from all the taps. Eventually Banjo discovers one behind the amenity block that's slowly leaking – *drip, drip, drip* – onto the path below. He kneels on the wet concrete to drink directly from the tap. It takes ages, but that doesn't matter; he's got all day. He's not in any hurry to go home.

Maybe he *won't* go home!

The idea pops into Banjo's head out of nowhere. And just as quickly, he dismisses it as ridiculous. Where would he go?

His knees are sore by the time he's finished drinking. It's not just from kneeling on the hard concrete; the insides of them look red and raw where they rubbed against the saddle all the way from the farm. He should have worn jeans. But today's a school day and jeans aren't part of the uniform.

Banjo wishes he was at school. He wishes none of this had happened. He wishes he'd caught the bus this morning, instead of staging his stupid Ride to School stunt. On the other hand, if he'd left Milly at home, the people from Gippsland would have driven away with her by now.

Zzzz zzzz zzzz! Someone is trying to phone him again. Banjo looks at his backpack lying on the path next to his helmet and Milly's saddle, where he dropped them at the corner of the building. It'll be one of his parents. He won't answer. They'll just ask where he and Milly are and come to get them.

And then hand Milly over to her new owners.

'*I'm* her owner!' Banjo shouts in the direction of his buzzing backpack, as if the caller can somehow hear him.

Where *is* Milly? he wonders. She must have wandered away while he was kneeling at the tap. He spots her eating grass down by the three saggy old clotheslines where the holiday-makers must have dried their washing. It's surprisingly green there. Banjo walks down to have a look. The ground seems damp. He turns and gazes back the way he has come. A line of dark, weedy soil wiggles its way up to the leaky tap. That explains it – months of slow seepage has produced this lush, grassy area at the bottom of the slope. Clever Milly to have found it.

Banjo removes her headgear. Nan taught him that you shouldn't let a horse eat with the bit in its mouth – it'll learn bad habits. 'When you take them out riding,' she explained, 'they'll stop for a nibble anytime they see something that looks tasty.'

'Also, it gives them wind,' she added and they both laughed.

Banjo smiles now, remembering. He misses Nan and Pop.

Leaving Milly to graze, he walks back up the slope and dumps her headgear on top of her saddle. He's hungry. He checks the time on his phone. It's only 11:15 am – way too early for lunch. But he had 'recess' early, so why not? There are no rules today. Biting into a sandwich, Banjo wonders if Milly's new owners are still waiting at the farm. Well, they'll just have to keep waiting. Maybe forever, ha ha. He takes another bite, trying not to swallow any of the swirling flies that settle back on the bread as quickly as he can shoo them off. When they were at primary school, Archie ate a fly once. Deliberately. He said it tasted like Vegemite. Archie is always doing crazy things like that. Yet this morning he had the nerve to call *Banjo* a mad dingo.

Is riding your horse to school as crazy as eating flies?

Banjo closes his lunch box, saving the second sandwich and the apple for later. He stands up and stretches. His leg muscles feel slightly sore from his long ride this morning. And the rubbed patches on the insides of his knees are worse than he thought.

They go halfway up his inner thighs. There are three large, weepy blisters.

And he still has to ride all the way home.

He'll worry about that later. Right now, he needs more water. But drinking from the leaky tap is agonisingly slow. Plus it hurts his knees. He needs to catch the drips somehow. Milly seems quite happy where she is – there's enough grass down by the clotheslines to keep her busy for a while – so Banjo leaves her there and goes searching for something to collect water in. He finds it soon enough. Someone has made a camp fire behind the wrecked caravan and left several empty stubbies lying in the ashes. Two are broken, but the rest are all right. Banjo selects the cleanest-looking one. It smells okay inside, just a bit ashy, but he wishes there was some way to clean it. Then he remembers the broken window at the Viganos' old house. Were there curtains? If there are, he could wet a strip of curtain fabric under the leaking tap, then wrap it around a stick and poke it into the bottle to clean the inside.

The house has a small backyard, surrounded by a metre-high fence. The gate squeals when Banjo opens it. He walks around the side to the broken window. There *are* curtains – yay! Banjo can't resist taking a peek in to see what's behind them. It's a big, empty bedroom with a doorway on one side that opens into an ensuite bathroom. Pushing the curtains sideways, Banjo can see partway into the ensuite. There's a slice of mirror, a corner of hand basin and a tap.

The tap still has its knob.

Banjo goes around to the Viganos' back door, but it's locked. So is the door that leads in through the office at the front of the building. He returns to the bedroom window. Is it wrong to go in? Nobody lives here. He just wants to see if the tap works. Reaching in through the large, star-shaped hole in the glass, Banjo undoes the latch and slides the creaky old window frame all the way up. Then he drops his bottle on the floor inside and carefully climbs in after it.

Both the taps over the handbasin still have their knobs. Banjo tries the cold one and – *woo hoo!* – water comes gurgling out. It's full of bubbles at first and slightly discoloured, but soon it runs clear. Frustratingly, his bottle won't fit under the tap unless he tips it sideways. Then it occurs to him that if the ensuite taps still have their knobs, the ones in the kitchen will, too.

A minute later, Banjo stands at the Viganos' kitchen sink, rinsing and re-rinsing his little brown bottle until he's satisfied it's clean. Then he fills it all the way to the top and drinks it all the way to the bottom. Beautiful!

Refilling his bottle for later, Banjo makes a quick tour of the house. There are two other bedrooms, a bathroom, a laundry, the office at the front and a small lounge room with dents in the carpet where the Viganos' furniture once stood. He tries a light switch, but nothing happens. The air smells old and musty. It's a bit creepy, actually; he can't wait to get back outside. It will be easier than coming in, Banjo thinks, because now that he's inside, he can unlock the doors. The back one is the obvious choice. It's in the laundry. He is about to open it when he notices a blue plastic bucket sitting upside down in the laundry trough.

Two minutes later, feeling pleased with himself, Banjo comes limping around the corner of the amenity block, bringing a bottle of water for himself and a bucket of water for Milly.

But Milly isn't there.

Banjo sets the bucket down, too heavily, next to Milly's saddle and a curl of water slops out onto the concrete. 'Where have you got to?' he asks the empty stretch of grass beneath the clotheslines where he last saw her.

He isn't worried, he knows where she'll be – down in the dry riverbed behind the caravan park, looking for water. If only she had waited a few more minutes, a bucket of clean, fresh water would have been delivered right to her.

'Silly Milly,' Banjo says.

Then he hears the distant blare of a car horn, a squeal of skidding tyres and the terrified whinny of a horse.

Dropping his bottle, Banjo spins around and goes sprinting up towards the road.

6

Famous

Two vehicles – a large white van and a little blue hatchback – have stopped about 300 metres past the caravan park. They are facing away from him. The van is closer than the hatchback, half blocking the road, with its hazard lights flashing.

Banjo's pounding feet carry him towards the scene of whatever has happened. His heart races, his mouth is dry. Somehow he is on the same side of the road as the two vehicles, although he has no recollection of crossing over. He can't see Milly. Perhaps he imagined the whinny. But he didn't imagine the car horn or the sound of skidding tyres.

The hatchback's passenger side door hangs open. Two women dressed in white (nurses?) are walking away from him along the gravel shoulder. He can't see what's down there – the van blocks his view. Its hazard lights are still flashing. A man gets out on the driver's side, closes the door and disappears around the front of the vehicle. Moments later, he reappears in front of Banjo. He hasn't seen Banjo yet – his face is turned away and he's speaking into a mobile phone.

'Excuse me!' Banjo calls breathlessly, running up behind him. 'What happened?'

The man turns his head, startled. He lowers his phone. 'Where did you spring from?' he asks curtly. Without waiting for an answer, he says, 'There's a horse on the road. They nearly hit it.'

Banjo's heart lifts at the word *nearly*. He still can't see past the van. 'Is the horse okay?'

'I think so,' says the man. He makes a see-for-yourself gesture with his phone hand. 'Is it yours?'

'Yes.' Banjo is so out of breath that it's hard to talk. It doesn't matter who Milly belongs to – him, his parents, or the people from Gippsland – as long as she's okay.

But he can see her now that he has reached the van and she is obviously *not* okay. She stands in the middle of the road about fifty metres ahead. There's a big blue and white tour bus coming from the other direction. Is it going to slow down? Milly looks panicky – her ears are flattened backwards and her tail is clamped down against her hindquarters. Who knows what she'll do if the bus driver sounds his air horn. One of the women in white edges nervously out onto the road towards Milly, one hand extended. Her companion looks on from the safety of the roadside.

'I'd better go and help,' gasps Banjo.

He jogs away from the man with the phone, who calls after him in a voice suddenly turned hostile, 'Your horse shouldn't be running around loose, buddy. I've reported it to the council.'

But his words barely register with Banjo, whose only concern is Milly. The nervous woman is talking to her, trying to calm her down.

'Aren't you a gorgeous, big horse,' she's saying as Banjo arrives.

He slides one arm under Milly's neck, strokes her whiskery muzzle with his other hand. 'Hey, Mills . . . *puff* . . . what are doing . . . *puff* . . . running around on the road . . . *puff* . . . getting in everyone's way?'

'Is it yours?' asks the woman.

'Yes.'

'It ran right in front of us. If Lynnie hadn't swerved, we would have run into it.'

'I'm sorry,' Banjo says. It's his fault that this happened – he shouldn't have left Milly and gone exploring the house.

He, Milly and the hatchback woman are still standing in the middle of the road. The bus has stopped about thirty metres away, with its big diesel engine throbbing. Thank you, driver, thinks Banjo. Taking a handful of Milly's mane, he guides her gently off the road.

The second woman, the one her friend called Lynnie, exclaims, 'Poor horse! Is it all right?'

'I think so.' Banjo nods. 'She's just a bit spooked. Thanks for not running into her.'

'Carol is the one you should be thanking,' Lynnie

tells him, indicating her friend. 'She's the brave one. She went out on the road to calm her down.'

'Thanks, both of you.' Banjo smiles at them. He recognises their white outfits now. They're not nurses, they're members of the Big River Lawn Bowls Club. Nan and Pop were members, too. Carol and Lynnie probably knew them, but he's not going to ask.

It might lead to another awkward conversation about why he isn't at school.

The tour bus blocks out half the sky as it edges slowly past, its far side tyres right over in the gravel to give the spooked horse and the three people tending to it as much space as possible. Banjo sends the driver a thank you wave. The passengers look like overseas tourists. They are probably on their way to Mungo National Park. Phones and cameras crowd against the glass as the big tinted windows scroll past. Images of the Australian boy and the horse that stopped the bus will be sent all over the world tonight.

We're going to be *famous*, Banjo thinks playfully.

How surprised he would be if he could see into the future.

7

Horse Catcher

Banjo takes his time leading Milly back towards the caravan park. He walks on the outside, shielding her as much as possible from the passing traffic. Luckily there isn't much traffic – it's early afternoon and most people are either at home having lunch or they're at work. But every time a car does go by, Milly tosses her head and shies away from him. She's still spooked after her close call with Lynnie and Carol's car. She lets Banjo know that she doesn't like him holding her mane – it must feel a bit like having your hair pulled. But he has no choice. He has to hold her somehow, otherwise she might run out onto the road again. And the next car mightn't stop as quickly as the blue hatchback did.

Fortunately, the caravan park is outside of the town boundary. It's a semi-rural area. There are no side streets to cross or hysterical town dogs to yap at Milly. Banjo walks her slowly along the gravel road shoulder, past a ravaged vineyard with its rows of fallen vines. Up ahead is a nursery and garden supplies centre with a big *Closing Down Sale* sign out front. Banjo must have run right past it on his way to find Milly, but he has no memory of it. All he remembers is the white van with its hazard lights flashing and the little blue hatchback with its door hanging open. He was so scared!

If anything had happened to Milly, Banjo would never forgive himself.

When a large white ute pulls up beside him, at first Banjo mistakes it for Tuan Le's – it's the same colour, the same model and it has the same council logo on the door. But behind the cab there's a difference. Instead of a water tank on the back, this one is fitted out with a large, boxed in cage. Uh-oh! It must be the dog catcher that Tuan warned him about, the one who's a stickler for rules.

Banjo wonders what rule he's breaking (apart from stealing his own horse and wagging school, ha ha!). Horses are allowed on the roadside, aren't they? He's not wearing a helmet, but Banjo is pretty sure that you have to be *on* a horse to need one.

The handbrake rasps on and an enormous, bald-headed man gets out. Usman's right, thinks Banjo, the guy *does* look like Jabba the Hutt!

'Is that your horse?' asks the Jabba lookalike.

'Yes.'

'Why is it running around loose?'

'She isn't loose,' Banjo points out. 'Look, I'm holding her.'

'I've had reports it was running loose on the road,'

insists Jabba. 'It nearly caused an accident.'

Now Banjo remembers the man from the white van telling him he'd called the council. But Van Man is long gone, as are Lynnie and Carol. There are no witnesses.

'Not *this* horse,' he says.

Jabba looks up and down the road. 'I don't see any others.'

Banjo doesn't say anything. He stands there stroking Milly's neck. Jabba knows he was lying, but there probably isn't a council rule about that.

'What's your name, kid?' asks Jabba.

'Archie,' Banjo hears himself say.

'Archie who?'

'Lawson.'

Jabba wears a council name badge like Tuan's; his name is Daryl Towers. But Jabba suits him better.

'And where do you live, Archie?' he asks.

It feels weird being called Archie. The real Archie will think this is the funniest thing in the world when he hears about it. But it doesn't feel funny right now to fake Archie, aka Banjo. He's digging a really deep hole for himself.

'Down there,' he says, pointing vaguely in the direction of town.

'How far?'

'A couple of kilometres.'

Jabba shoos away a fly. 'So what are you and your horse doing here? Shouldn't you be at school?'

Banjo can't think of an explanation that will be even half-believable. He's not very good at lying. He strokes Milly's neck and tells a version of the truth. 'She ran away and I chased after her.'

Jabba nods. 'I suppose you realise there's a fine for letting a horse run around loose?'

'Someone left the gate open,' Banjo says, back to lying again. 'It wasn't my fault.'

'It's the owner's responsibility to make sure gates *aren't* left open,' Jabba informs him. He looks Banjo up and down. 'Or your parents' responsibility, in this case.'

'She's my horse,' says Banjo. He doesn't want his parents to find out about this. 'How much is the fine?'

'Two hundred and fifty dollars.' Jabba smiles as he says this. 'That's for the council by-laws infringement. But I expect there'll be another charge for the traffic incident,' he adds. 'I'll leave that one for the police to sort out.'

Banjo stands in dazed silence as Jabba waddles back to his ute and opens a steel locker on the side of the cage.

The police, he thinks numbly. This just gets worse and worse!

Jabba returns with a big coil of rope with a padded loop on one end – it's a halter rope. He has come prepared. 'Put this on him,' he says, passing the rope to Banjo.

Banjo slips the loop over Milly's head. She snorts

and does a little sideways dance, tugging on the rope. 'Easy, girl,' he says soothingly, stroking her with his free hand.

Jabba has backed off a few paces. He is obviously not a horse person. 'Do your parents have a horse trailer?' he asks.

'Yes.'

'That makes it easier.' Jabba pulls out his phone. 'Give me your dad or your mum's number and I'll get one of them to come and collect him.'

Banjo realises his mistake. He should have lied about the horse trailer. 'They are both at work,' he says.

Jabba looks him in the eye. 'There are two ways we can do this, Archie. Either your parents come and collect him, or I arrange for someone else to do it. But there'd be a charge for that – I think it's about $300.'

Banjo does the maths: $250 for the by-laws infringement + $300 for taking Milly home = $550. And there might even be some sort of traffic fine on top of that, if the police *do* become involved. Banjo's parents are the ones who will have to pay, because he doesn't have that kind of money.

His parents might not have that kind of money, either, Banjo realises. Financially, things are certainly not good on the farm.

'Why not let *me* take her home, Mr Towers,' he tries to reason with him. 'It isn't far. I've got a rope now. Tell me where you work and I'll bring it back afterwards.'

Jabba sighs. 'This is an official matter, Archie. A complaint was phoned in and I was sent to sort it out. I can't just turn my back and pretend that nothing's happened. Now, give me that number.'

'What number?' asks Banjo, playing dumb.

'Your mum's or your dad's.'

'But you said you were going to call someone else to come and get my horse.'

The stickler-for-rules Council Bylaws Officer looks Banjo up and down, no doubt recognising the uniform of the town's only high school. 'How old are you?' he asks.

'Seventeen,' says Banjo, adding a couple of years. But he's big for his age.

Jabba shakes his head. 'If you were eighteen, it would be different,' he says. 'But since you're a minor, I'll need to get your parents' authorisation before I go ahead and make those arrangements.'

'They're at work,' Banjo insists.

'You told me that,' Jabba reminds him. 'But unless they work on the International Space Station, I'm sure there must be a number that will reach them.'

The game is up. Banjo knows his parents will find out about this sooner or later, but he was hoping for later. If Jabba calls them now, at least they'll have the chance to avoid the extra $350 horse transport fee by coming to collect Milly in her own trailer. He is about to give the dog/horse-catcher his mother's number when Jabba's phone rings.

'Hi Lana,' Jabba answers. He listens for a moment. 'How serious is it? . . . Did they catch the other dog? . . . Okay, I'd better get over there . . . Listen, I'll need someone to take over for me here . . . Out on Burgess Road . . . Yes, the horse . . . No, not Tuan, Matthew would be better . . . Fine. Ask him to jump in his car and come straight over.'

With the phone still clamped to his ear, Jabba turns and looks in the direction of the nursery with the *Closing Down Sale* notice out front. 'Tell Matthew to come to the carpark outside Burgess Plants and Gardens,' he says. 'I'll call him from the truck and fill him in on what's going on . . . Yes, there's a kid with the horse . . . high school age . . . I'll get him to wait for Matthew . . . Thanks, Lana. Bye.'

Jabba lowers his phone and turns to Banjo. 'I have to go. What I want you to do is take your horse down to that garden supplies shop over there' – he points – 'and wait in the carpark out front for a guy called Matthew Turpin. He should be there in about ten minutes.'

'How will I recognise him?' asks Banjo.

'He'll be in a white council car. But don't worry, he'll find you.' As he's speaking, Jabba has waddled around the other side of his ute and opened the driver's door. He pauses before getting in, points a fat finger across the roof at Banjo and issues a stern warning, 'Don't even *think* about running off before Matthew arrives, Archie. I know who you are.'

No you don't! thinks fake Archie Lawson.

8

Thirty Seconds

Banjo doesn't go to the nursery to wait for the Matthew guy to arrive. Instead, he takes Milly directly back to the caravan park. But he no longer feels safe there. Only 150 metres down the road from the nursery, it will be the first place anyone looks if they come searching for a boy and a horse.

Collecting his backpack and Milly's riding gear from behind the amenity block, Banjo leads her down through the dry riverbed and up into the narrow strip of forest on the other side. There's lots of cover here, no one will find them. But there isn't much shade because most of the trees are drought-stressed like the Canoe Tree – more leaves litter the ground than remain on their peeling branches. If only horses ate gum leaves, he thinks. There's nothing here for Milly to eat. Banjo knows she'd much rather be back at the caravan park, grazing on the lush green grass beneath the clotheslines, but it's no longer safe. He's glad he has the halter. Thank you, Jabba. The rope is longer than he thought – fully unwound, it extends at least 10 metres from the metal swivel where it connects to the neck collar. Banjo tethers Milly to a slim, smooth-barked sapling, then he sits on the hard, dusty ground and leans back against Milly's saddle. It makes a comfortable backrest. Much more comfortable, Banjo thinks, than if he was sitting *on* it. The insides of his knees are rubbed raw – how is he ever going to ride all the way home again? Banjo eats the rest of his lunch slowly while he tries to work out what to do.

He should phone his parents. They will be going nuts by now. But it serves them right – they shouldn't have sold Milly. She's *his* horse.

He's not going to take her back!

That's a silly thought. He and Milly will have to go home *some* time. Just not yet. He'll let his parents stew for a bit longer. Crunching into his apple, he checks the time on his phone. It's 1:01 pm. The lunch bell will have just rung. Everyone will be filing out of their classes. Will his friends be talking about him?

He shouldn't have said he was Archie Lawson. What was he thinking? If he was going to lie about it, he should have made up a name – Billy Brown or something. Is it identity theft to use someone else's name? It hardly matters – Banjo has done so many wrong things today that one more hardly makes a difference.

The only wrong thing he *doesn't* regret is taking Milly.

He wonders if Jabba has phoned the school yet.

That's what he'll do when he finds out the high school kid calling himself Archie Lawson didn't wait for the Matthew guy at the nursery. Jabba will ask the office lady if a student with that name attends Big River High School. She will put him through to Mr Gunston, who will check and say that Archie has been at school all day. Then Mr Gunston will tell Jabba about another boy, one who came to school that morning on a horse and then went AWOL.

Sprung!

Banjo looks at his phone. There are now nine missed calls. One is from the landline at home – his father, obviously – and eight are from his mother. She has left two more voice messages, but he's not going to listen to them. His phone needs recharging. He switches it off to save the battery. He'll turn it back on later and call his mother to say he's coming home. Or he might just send a text message, that would be easier.

He puts the phone and his empty lunchbox back into his school bag. It's hot in the broken shade of the thirsty gum trees. Banjo is thirsty, too. As is Milly. He can't take her to get a drink because someone might see her if he brings her out of the trees. A boy is much less likely to be seen than a horse. Leaving Milly tied to the sapling, Banjo crosses the riverbed back towards the caravan park, moving quickly, his eyes darting back and forth. He feels like a teenage runaway in a movie, only this isn't a movie. A minute later he crosses back in the other direction, this time carrying a brown glass bottle and blue bucket.

Banjo sips from his bottle while Milly drinks from the bucket. He finishes first, but the big thirsty mare is not far behind. She bumps the empty bucket along the ground, trying to get every last drop. The bucket tips over. Banjo picks it up and tickles the side of Milly's water-beaded muzzle.

'Still thirsty?' he asks. 'So am I. Wait here.'

Taking the empty bottle and the empty bucket, Banjo hurries back to the caravan park. There's no problem getting into the Viganos' house this time; he left the back door unlocked. He places the bucket in the laundry trough and cranks open the cold tap. When the bucket is three-quarters full, he slides it to one side and fills his bottle. *Overfills* it – he should have adjusted the flow. Water surges out over his hand and splatters noisily into the trough. It sounds like rain on an iron roof, something Banjo hasn't heard for who knows how long.

It was a lovely sound then, but today, in the Viganos' old laundry, it's just the noise of water being wasted. Banjo quickly turns off the tap. When you've lived this long in a drought, you know how precious water is. He should tell someone about the leaking tap behind the amenity block, so they can get it fixed. Who owns the caravan park now that the Viganos have gone? he wonders. His parents might know – he'll ask them tonight.

He's not in any hurry to go home. The longer he leaves it, the less chance there is that those people from Gippsland will still be there. Plus, the insides of Banjo's knees and thighs are too sore for another 21 kilometres in the saddle wearing only shorts. He needs to get a pair of jeans or trousers from somewhere.

Archie, he thinks. I'll wait till school's out, then give him a call.

While he's having these thoughts, Banjo has taken a sip from his overfilled bottle. Fresh from the tap, the water is so cool and delicious that he has another sip. Before he realises it, the bottle is half empty. Banjo uses the back of his left wrist to wipe a dribble of water off his chin. So good! This time when he refills the bottle, he is careful not to turn the tap on too hard.

It took perhaps 30 seconds to drink from the bottle, wipe his chin and fill the bottle again – a tiny delay. But those extra 30 seconds spent in the Viganos' laundry are to have a life-changing effect on Banjo's future.

And a lot of other people's lives will be changed by it, too.

9

Too Close for Comfort

Banjo's hand freezes on the doorknob when he hears the crunch of tyres outside. It's a sound he has heard more than once today, but this time it makes his heart race. Placing the heavy bucket gently on the laundry floor, he peeps out through a tiny gap between the spider-webbed curtain and the window frame. Just as he feared, it's a big white council ute with a closed-in cage on the back. Jabba's big, boofy head swivels from side to side as he drives slowly past the Viganos' old house. Banjo ducks out of sight. That was too close for comfort. Had Jabba come along only thirty seconds later, Banjo would have been outside, in full view. Game over.

But it isn't a game and nor is it over. Jabba is still out there, patrolling the caravan park, looking for him and Milly. What if he goes down to the grassy area near the clotheslines and sees that a horse has been there? Milly's hooves will have left telltale prints in the soggy ground. And she has probably left other evidence, as well – what goes in, must come out. But even if Jabba sees that Milly has been there, he won't find her. He'll think fake Archie and his horse are long gone. It won't occur to him to look in the Viganos' house. But Banjo locks the laundry door anyway, just in case. Then he goes through to the master bedroom, where there is a better view from the window. He is rewarded, less than a minute later, by the sight of Jabba's ute driving back up the far side of the caravan park towards Burgess Road. Phew! If the stickler-for-the-rules Council Bylaws Officer had seen anything suspicious, he wouldn't be leaving so quickly.

Second round to Banjo.

10

Runaway Schoolkid

Call me. URGENT! Don't tell ANYONE!!!

Banjo presses Send. It's 2:51 pm. He waited 20 minutes so Archie wouldn't get his message while he was still at school. If any of their friends were nearby, Archie wouldn't be able to help himself. 'Guess who just sent me a text?' he'd say. Archie isn't very good at keeping secrets.

Banjo takes a small sip from his bottle. He's back in their hiding place, resting against Milly's saddle in the strip of forest across from the caravan park. Milly stands a few metres away, with her head down. Every so often she blinks or swishes her tail when a fly bothers her, but otherwise she doesn't move. About an hour ago, Banjo crossed the river and filled his backpack with ripped-up grass from beneath the clotheslines. But when he emptied it in front of Milly, she just sniffed it and refused to eat. She's sulking. She doesn't like being tethered. But Banjo can't risk releasing her – she might run off again. Poor Milly.

It has been a long, boring afternoon for both of them. The minutes have seemed like hours. Banjo must have switched on his phone 50 times to check the time. Well, maybe not 50. Each time used up more of the phone's dwindling battery life. Now it reads just 2%. But he leaves it turned on, hoping Archie will get his message soon.

Archie, check your phone, you slacker! he thinks.

Even though he's expecting it, when the screen suddenly lights up and the phone does ring, Banjo is taken by surprise. He answers it.

'I ought to kill you!' are the first words Archie says. But he's laughing as he speaks. 'You'll never believe what happened! At lunchtime, Mr Gunston dragged me into his office and –'

Banjo cuts him off. 'Archie, listen up. My phone's about to die, we have to make this quick. Can you come and meet me?'

'Sure. Where are you?'

'First you have to promise not to tell anyone.'

'Promise,' says Archie.

Banjo gives directions. Then he asks Archie to bring a couple of things.

Archie is taking forever to get there. Watching from behind a big dead rivergum on the other side of the river, Banjo begins to wonder if his friend has gone to the wrong place. Are there two caravan parks in Big River? He can't call Archie to check, because now his phone is totally dead. It won't even tell him what time it is. The sun has moved quite a long way down the sky; it must be nearly five o'clock. On a normal school day, Banjo would be home by now. If his father was working near the house, they might have afternoon tea together. Or Banjo would fix himself a drink and a snack, then play on the computer for half an hour before starting his homework. Sometimes that half-hour stretched on a bit longer. It occurs to Banjo now that he could have spent some of that wasted time with Milly. He promised Nan he would take her – now *his* – horse out for a ride every day. He wishes he'd kept that promise. His parents would have noticed. Things might have turned out differently.

There's movement across the river. At last! Archie comes weaving his bicycle down the main gravel track between the empty caravan sites. What took him so long? Banjo is about to step out into the open and wave, when a second cyclist comes into view about 20 metres behind the one he assumed was Archie, but now isn't sure. Both cyclists are wearing helmets and it's difficult to see who they are from this distance. Is *either* of them Archie?

They stop at the corner of the amenity block and let their bikes drop onto the ground. It must be Archie – Banjo asked him to meet him in exactly that spot. The two figures remove their helmets. Now they are recognisable. It's Archie, all right, but he has brought Usman with him. Banjo can't believe it. Well, he *can* believe it, Archie being who he is. Banjo should have called someone else if he wanted total secrecy.

He just hopes Archie hasn't blabbed to everyone.

His two friends stand at the corner of the amenity block, their heads swivelling back and forth. Banjo's second choice of someone to call for help would have been Usman, who *wouldn't* have blabbed. But there wasn't a choice really; Banjo couldn't *not* call Archie after stealing his identity earlier today. He steps out from behind the big, dead tree and waves. Usman sees him first, says something to Archie and points.

'What are you doing over there?' yells Archie.

Banjo makes shushing gestures with his hands as he crosses the empty river towards them, jogging to close the distance quickly so no more shouting will be necessary.

'Hey, Archie, my man!' Usman greets him with a high five.

Banjo is confused for a moment, wondering why Usman called him Archie. Then he gets it and laughs.

'What's with the dobbing me in bulldust?' the real Archie asks. 'Some council dude actually rang my mum and accused me of horse theft.'

'Sorry.' Banjo grins sheepishly. 'That must have been Jabba. He asked —'

'Jabba?' Archie interrupts.

'The dog catcher,' Banjo explains. He turns to Usman. 'It was the same guy who nabbed Susie. He *does* look like Jabba the Hutt!'

'Ugly dude,' agrees Usman. 'Did he get your horse?'

'No. But he was going to hit me with all these fines,' Banjo says. 'He even said he was going to get the police in on the action. So when he asked my name, I just said the first thing that came into my head.'

'Thanks for thinking of me,' Archie says dryly.

'You should feel honoured. I could have said Liam Coleman.'

They all laugh. Liam is the smartest kid in Year 9, but he's a bit of loser.

Banjo continues, 'I knew it wouldn't get you in trouble, Arch. You don't even own a horse.'

Archie turns in a circle. He's wearing a backpack – not the one he takes to school, but a larger one with a Cronulla Sharks logo on the main panel. It looks quite full. 'Where *is* Milly?' he asks.

Banjo points across the river. 'In the trees over there. We were hiding out in case Jabba came back. Did you bring food?'

Archie slips the backpack off his shoulders and unzips it. 'I have your order here, sir.' With a flourish, he removes three crinkly packages from the front compartment. 'We have . . . let me see: salt and vinegar, barbecue and . . . yeah, another salt and vinegar. Take your pick.'

Potato chips. Banjo was hoping for something more filling. He's starving. He selects one of the salt and vinegars and tears the packet open with his teeth.

'Thanks, Arch,' he remembers to say, almost too late.

His friend nods. 'That's four dollars fifty, but you can pay me some other time.'

Banjo is surprised. If the situation were reversed, he wouldn't ask for money. His mouth is full of crunched-up potato fragments, but he talks around them, 'My wallet's in my schoolbag, over where Milly is.'

'Just kidding,' says Archie. He keeps one of the other packets and tosses the last one to Usman. 'These come compliments of Usman's dad,' he tells Banjo.

Banjo nearly chokes. 'You told *him*, as well?'

'Course not. It's the basketball breakup tonight. I was over at Ussy's helping set things up. That's why we took so long.'

Banjo had forgotten about the basketball breakup. Usman's father is the coach. They are having a barbecue tonight and everyone is sleeping over afterwards in the Farookis' big shed. Banjo was invited, but he wasn't in the team this season, so it didn't seem right to go. Last year, he was their second highest goal scorer. His and Archie's parents used to take turns driving them to practice every second Tuesday night and to their games on Thursdays, but when the Lawsons moved to town, the prospect of all that extra driving, plus the cost of petrol, was too much for Banjo's parents.

My life sucks, he thinks.

He asks, 'Did you bring the other stuff?'

'Think I remembered everything.' Archie places his bag of chips on the strip of concrete behind the amenity block. Then, unzipping the main compartment of his backpack, he produces a pair of jeans, a blue hoodie and a box of band-aids. He sets them down in a tidy row on the concrete, placing the band-aids on top of the flattened backpack. With Archie's unopened bag of chips at one end, it looks like a display of items on sale at a Sunday market.

Archie picks up his chips, spoiling the effect. 'Why do you want the plasters?'

Banjo turns his legs out so his friends can see the pink, weepy skin on the insides of his knees. 'Saddle rub,' he explains. 'Comes from wearing shorts when you ride a horse all the way from my place to school.'

'You were supposed to ride a bike, dummy, not a horse,' says Archie.

Banjo crunches the last of his chips. 'Would you ride your bike twenty-one kilometres?' he asks.

'No. I'd have caught the bus.'

'It was *ride* to school day.'

'You *ride* in a bus,' points out Archie.

'You're starting to sound like Liam Coleman,' Banjo tells him. 'No wonder you moved to town.' Then he realises what he just said – Archie's family moved to town because they went broke and had to sell their farm. 'Sorry, I didn't mean that.'

'Mean what?'

'That you're like Liam,' Banjo says quickly. Nice save.

Archie grins. 'I *am* like Liam. Today I aced Mr Turbot's maths quiz.'

'You did not.'

'He did,' Usman confirms. 'But it was an easy one. Half the class got them all right. One of the questions was about you.'

'Yeah, sure!' scoffs Banjo.

Usman turns to Archie. 'Can you remember how it went?'

Archie looks thoughtful. 'Something like: If X rides a bicycle at 12 kilometres per hour and B rides a horse at 40 kilometres per hour, who will get to school first?'

'B, obviously,' Banjo says. 'Now I know you're making it up – that's way too easy for one of Turbo's quizzes.'

'Archie left stuff out,' explains Usman. 'X lived closer to school than you.'

'Than me?'

'Turbo didn't say it was you, but it was pretty obvious who B was.'

'So who did get to school first?' Banjo asks, interested.

'X.'

'Oh.' Banjo feels genuinely disappointed. 'Hey, you guys aren't pulling my chain, are you?'

'No,' says Archie. 'X got there first.'

Banjo rolls his eyes. 'Not about the answer, about the whole thing. Was there really a quiz question about B on a horse?'

Usman nods seriously. 'It's totally true, Banj. You're famous. Everyone at school was talking about you.'

'Including Mr Gunston when I got dragged into his office,' adds Archie. He tosses a chip into the air and tries to catch it in his mouth, but misses. 'I still can't believe you told that Jabba guy you were me.'

'Next time I'll say I'm Liam, I promise.'

They all laugh. Liam's mother is a lawyer. And if she's anything like her son, Banjo thinks, she would probably take him to court for defamation. He might end up in court anyway. This hasn't been a very good day. Until now.

'Tell us what happened with Jabba,' Usman prompts him.

So Banjo tells the whole story. It seems funny now and he exaggerates a bit. When he gets to the end, Archie and Usman are laughing so hard they nearly choke on their chips.

While he waits for them to settle down, Banjo's spike of happiness slowly flattens down. 'Do you think Jabba *will* report me to the police?' he asks.

'Probably not,' says Archie. 'Guys like that get off on making threats and big-noting themselves. My guess is he'll keep quiet about the whole thing because he's embarrassed you got away.'

'He went to the school, though,' Banjo says.

'He *rang* the school,' Archie corrects him. 'But he was looking for a guy named Archie Lawson, not Banjo Tully. You totally fooled him! And you made a fool *of* him. He won't want the police to know about that.'

Banjo feels better, but only a tiny bit. His main concern now is about going home – about the reception he'll get from his parents. Unlike Jabba, they won't want to sweep this whole thing under the carpet.

'Is there more food?' he asks.

'Fraid not,' Archixe says, his words shooting out crumbs. 'I only brought three packets.'

One packet each. Banjo watches his two friends crunching away on their chips. It doesn't seem fair. After this, they'll both be going back to the basketball breakup at Usman's, where there will be more food than anyone can eat. And Banjo will be left here on his own. With absolutely *no* food.

He picks up the jeans Archie brought and holds them up against himself. The legs seem a bit short, but they will probably fit. He can try them on later, after his friends have gone. He will have to stick band-aids on the insides of his knees first, to stop any more rubbing. Even so, he isn't looking forward to getting back in the saddle. There are a lot of things he isn't looking forward to. It's better not to think about them.

Banjo picks up the hoodie, which is nice and big.

He slips it on over his short-sleeved school shirt and pulls the hood up. Nobody will take a second look at him now – he won't look like a runaway schoolkid.

Archie has finally finished his chips. He asks, 'Will you get home before dark?'

'I'm not going home tonight,' Banjo says, surprising himself. He has been toying with the idea all afternoon, but he didn't make the decision until the words came out of his mouth just now.

Archie is surprised too. 'What are you going to do?'

'Stay here,' says Banjo.

'*Here?*' Archie and Usman both say together.

'In the Viganos' old house,' he tells them. 'Remember Sebastian Vigano from primary school? He had a little sister, too. Their family ran this place. You would have passed their old house on the way in. Nobody lives there now.'

'Have you got a key?' Usman asks doubtfully.

'The back door isn't locked.'

'Cool!' says Archie. 'Let's go and take a look around.'

They spend three or four minutes exploring the house. Banjo's friends are impressed. They go from room to room, flicking light switches, opening and closing curtains, looking in cupboards and wardrobes. They exclaim loudly at each new discovery. You would think they had never seen a flushing toilet before!

Finally, they all end up in the Viganos' lounge

room, the only room in the house with carpet. Archie lies on his back in the middle of the floor, as if testing it for comfort. He even closes his eyes.

'Not too bad,' he says dreamily. 'But we'll need sleeping bags.'

Banjo and Usman look at each other, eyebrows raised.

'What?' says Archie, eyes open again, seeing their expressions. 'You don't think I'd let you stay here all on your lonesome, do you, Tully?'

11

If Ever It Rains Again

It doesn't take them long to work things out. Usman can't stay the night because the basketball breakup is at his place and his parents would soon notice if he wasn't there. But Archie can slip away when everyone's eating. The Under-14s are going to be there too – that's a lot of kids. One less won't make any difference. If anyone asks about Archie, Usman will cover for him.

Banjo stands at the corner of the amenity block, watching his two friends ride up through the caravan park towards the road. Archie wears his Cronulla Sharks backpack. It's empty now, but it will come back full. He has promised to bring food – '*Proper* food this time,' Banjo insisted, 'not chips' – as well as two sleeping bags. Archie said he'd be as quick as he could, but that he might not return till after dark. The days are getting shorter now and there is little more than an hour of daylight left. It doesn't give Banjo much time for what *he* has to do.

He crosses the river to get Milly first. As soon as she sees him coming through the trees, she nickers softly and comes to greet him, pulling her rope taut. Banjo lets her nuzzle his chest with her big salty-smelling head as he strokes behind her ears. Sometimes Nan used to kiss her when they greeted each other, but he's not Nan. She was a kinder horse owner than Banjo. A better one, too. The blue bucket has tipped over and there's a dark patch around it where the water spilled out. The grass he brought over earlier has been trodden into the dirt.

'Sorry, Mills,' Banjo says, as he unties the rope.

It must be five o'clock by now. Jabba will have knocked off and gone home, so it's safe to bring Milly back to the caravan park. She starts grazing as soon as they reach the grassy area by the clotheslines. Banjo tethers her to one of the clothesline poles and goes back across the river for the bucket and his backpack. He doesn't bother with Milly's saddle and headgear; he can fetch them later. Filling the bucket in the Viganos' laundry, he carries it down to her. She takes a long drink, then returns to grazing. Banjo notices there isn't much grass left. She has chomped most of it down almost to ground level.

The plant nursery had better be open.

Banjo removes his wallet from his backpack and opens it to check how much money he brought to school today. Well, technically not *to* school. There's five dollars and a few silver coins. Will that be enough? A sign outside the nursery said everything was half-price. The normal price for a bale of hay wouldn't be more than ten dollars.

Archie's jeans fit him okay. The thick denim burns the insides of his knees where the skin's blistered, but there isn't time to take them off again and stick on some band-aids because he's not sure how long the nursery will stay open. Following the same route his two friends took on their bicycles, Banjo makes his way towards the caravan park's entrance. They should be nearly at Usman's by now. He hopes Archie can keep his mouth shut. It would totally suck if the entire basketball team learned where he is. Secrecy's the thing. Just before he reaches Burgess Road, Banjo pulls the hood of his borrowed windcheater all the way forward until it half-covers his face. *Runaway schoolkid* sounds kind of cool. But he isn't really running away, he's just keeping his head down until tomorrow.

He'll go home in the morning.

The plant nursery *is* still open. Phew! When he and Milly walked past a few hours ago, shortly after his run-in with Jabba, Banjo glanced into the carpark where he was supposed to wait for the Matthew-guy and something caught his eye – a small stack of hay bales over in the far corner.

Perhaps a dozen vehicles are here now. People must have come after work to grab last minute Closing Down Sale bargains. An elderly couple loads an assortment of vegetable seedlings into the back of a red Rav 4. A younger man pushes a brand new wheelbarrow half-filled with shiny garden tools. Two women carry a matching pair of swaying ferns in matching green pots. Banjo has to detour around a dented old farm truck to make sure the hay bales are still there. The stack looks smaller than it did earlier, but he only needs one. Adjusting his hood, he turns and walks inside.

It's quite busy in the cluttered sales area – there are lots of bargain hunters. Careful not to make eye contact with anyone, Banjo makes his way purposefully towards the sales counter. Ahead of him, a skinny old man about Pop's age talks to a friendly-faced woman wearing a green shirt with *Burgess Plants & Gardens* embroidered on the pocket. The old man is buying a roll of chicken wire. Banjo hangs back a couple of metres, but he can hear their conversation.

'I'm sorry to hear you are shutting down.'

'It's a sign of the times. Who can keep a garden going since they put the water restrictions up to Level Five?'

They begin talking about the drought and how it's caused by climate change, at which point Banjo tunes out. He picks up a random item from the One Dollar table and pretends to study it. It's a clear plastic cylinder with an open top and little numbers running down the side.

'Know what that's for?'

Banjo jumps. A very tall man looms over him.

He must be well over two metres and wears a green *Burgess Plants & Gardens* shirt like the woman's.

'To measure liquid?' Banjo guesses.

'You got it, bud – it's for measuring rainfall.' The tall man smiles. 'You can have it for nothing.'

'It says one dollar.'

'It's a freebie. Take it home and attach it to your fence. Who knows, one day some rain might even fall in it!'

Banjo is embarrassed. The tall man has a loud voice. Both the woman behind the counter and the old man have stopped their own conversation to listen. All three adults are smiling at him now. He feels silly hiding under the hood, so he pushes it back off his head.

'Thanks,' he says.

The woman calls out, 'There should be a holder for that rain gauge, Gerry.'

Gerry, the tall, loud man, rummages through the items on the bargain table and finds a black plastic bracket, which he hands to Banjo. 'You put screws through those two holes. Don't use nails, bud, you might break it.'

Banjo nods and thanks him again.

'Is there anything else I can help you with?' asks Gerry.

'Yes. How much are the hay bales?'

'Hay bales?'

'Out the front.' Banjo points. 'There's a stack of

them out there near the fence.'

'That's not hay, it's straw,' Gerry corrects him.

Banjo feels his face turn red. He should have known that. This is a nursery – it sells stuff for gardens, not for animals. Horses don't eat straw. 'Okay. Well, thanks again for this,' he stammers, holding up the rain gauge as he turns to walk away.

'Why do you want hay?' Gerry's big voice follows him.

Banjo wants to keep walking, but that would be rude. He stops and turns around. 'For a horse.'

'To eat?'

Banjo nods. Why else would a horse want hay? When he came in here, he had hoped not to attract attention. Now everybody is looking at him.

'Well, sorry I can't help you there, bud.' Gerry gives him an exaggerated wink. 'But at least you're all set up with that gauge if ever it rains again.'

If ever it rains again. Banjo doesn't know how many times he has heard those five words repeated over the past few years. There's a standard, two-word reply:

'What's rain?' he asks and everyone in the sales area laughs, as if he has just made the funniest joke in the world.

But it isn't funny at all.

12

Silver Lining

Banjo is almost back to the caravan park when a dented old farm truck pulls off the road onto the gravel beside him. It's the old man who was buying chicken wire at the nursery. He's motioning at Banjo to get in.

Banjo walks to the truck's open passenger side window. 'It's okay, I don't need a lift, thanks.'

'That isn't why I stopped,' the old man says. 'Would chaff do?'

'I beg your pardon?'

'You wanted food for your horse – would it like some chaff?'

Nan used to give chaff to Milly sometimes. She would mix it in with Milly's oats or horse pellets after jumping events.

'I guess so,' he says.

'That's not a very enthusiastic answer, Sonny Jim.' The old man seems offended. 'I'm not suggesting you *pay* for it.'

Banjo realises he wasn't very polite. 'Sorry. Yes, some chaff would be great. Thank you.'

'Hop in then.'

All his life it's been drummed into Banjo not to accept lifts from strangers. But he's fifteen now, big for his age and probably much stronger than the skinny old man in the truck. Besides, Milly will need *something* to eat if they're staying overnight at the caravan park – the grass down by the clotheslines was nearly all gone when he left.

'Do you have a horse?' Banjo asks as they drive off.

The old man chuckles. 'Horses are a bit beyond me now. But my great-granddaughter used to have a Shetland pony. It lived in my back paddock until Matilda and her parents moved up to Newcastle. They left a couple of bags of chaff in my shed when they went.'

'When was that?' asks Banjo. Chaff starts to go mouldy if you keep it too long.

'Last November,' the old man says. 'Do you remember the Black Billy Tearooms?'

'Across the road from IGA?'

'That's the place. My granddaughter and her husband – Matilda's parents – owned it. They had to close down last year, thanks to this infernal drought.'

Banjo runs his fingers up and down the bumpy millimetre markers on the outside of his rain gauge. 'How can the drought cause a tea place to close?' he asks.

The old man makes a bubbly throat-clearing noise

before he speaks. 'Two things keep this town afloat, son – agriculture and tourism – and the drought is slowly killing them both.'

'I saw a tourist bus today.'

'If it stopped here in town,' the old man says sadly, 'it would only have been to use the rest rooms. Then they'd have gone on to Mildura or Mungo Park or . . . or to Timbuktu. This used to be a holiday town – people came here from all over for our river. They'd spend money in our shops and cafes and everybody would benefit. Not anymore. The poor sods who own businesses are barely making enough to pay their rent.'

Banjo isn't sure what to say. Apart from that one time when he saw Mr and Mrs Vigano on *60 Minutes*, he hasn't given much thought to what the drought might mean to people who don't live on farms. It certainly isn't something he and his friends talk about. 'I'm sorry about your great-granddaughter's family,' he says.

The old man laughs. 'Well, at least there's a silver lining, sonny. Your horse gets a free dinner!'

There are two large bags. The labels say Lucerne Chaff. One is already open. The old man scoops some out and sniffs it.

'Could be a bit stale,' he says. 'What do you think, son?'

Banjo takes a handful and lifts it to his nose. There's a faint, musty smell. 'I'm not sure.'

They are standing in a big shed at the side of the old man's house. The single overhead light is switched on, but it's shrouded in cobwebs and the shed is dim. Banjo takes his crumbly handful of chaff outside for a better look. The sun has just gone down, but it's much lighter out here than inside.

'I think it's going mouldy,' he agrees.

The old man has followed him as far as the doorway. 'That's a pity. The other bag might be all right though – it hasn't been opened.'

According to the label, the full bag weighs 25 kilos. It's too heavy for the old man to lift. He watches Banjo heave it up onto the back of the truck.

'Where do you live, son?' he asks.

'Way out of town. Could you drop me back where you picked me up? Dad's coming to get me.'

They drive back the way they came. The old man talks wistfully about his great-granddaughter. Matilda used to come and ride her Shetland pony every Saturday afternoon and afterwards her parents would drive him back to their place for dinner. It's obvious he misses them. He doesn't ask Banjo anything about himself or why he's in town late on a Friday afternoon trying to find food for his horse. Banjo is relieved. He's a nice old man and it feels awful to lie to him. But some lies can't be avoided.

'Dad said he'd pick me up out the front of the caravan park,' he says, just as they are about to drive past it. He waited until the last moment on purpose, so the old man won't have time to wonder why Banjo and his father have made such an unlikely arrangement. If Banjo *had* found a bale of hay at the nursery, how would he have moved it 150 metres from the nursery to the caravan park? Hay bales are almost impossible to carry.

It's only after he's said goodbye to the old man and the truck's tail lights are just two tiny red dots in the distance, that Banjo remembers he left the rain gauge on the front seat. Well, he had no use for it anyway – *What's rain? Ha ha!* The last glow of daylight is rapidly fading behind the trees as he drags the heavy bag of chaff into the caravan park. Leaving it outside the Viganos' back fence, he goes to get Milly.

'I've got you some dinner, Mills,' Banjo tells her as he unties her rope from the middle clothesline.

Leading her up to the house, he opens the little gate and sets her free in the backyard. The fence is quite low, but she won't try to escape as long as she has food and water. Banjo will go back for her bucket in a minute; her food comes first. He drags the chaff in through the gate and tries to open the bag. But it's sewn firmly closed across the top and he can't make a hole with his fingernails. He wishes he'd thought about this before the old man dropped him off. If Matilda's great-grandfather was anything like Pop, he would have a pocketknife in the glove box or somewhere else in his truck.

Banjo misses his grandparents. He misses everyone.

He wishes he was at home.

But if he was at home, where would Milly be?

'I can't believe they tried to sell you, Mills,' he says for the umpteenth time.

She's standing over him, breathing loudly into his hair – *whuff whuff whuff* – as he struggles to open the bag. It tickles the back of his neck and he pulls the hood up.

And because he's bent over the bag in the fading daylight, with the hood closed around him like a narrow-mouthed cave and Milly's loud breathing the only noise in his world, Banjo is unaware of a small, blue-white light that comes wobbling around the corner of the house and the scratch of narrow tyres on gravel.

'What are you doing?'

Startled by the sudden and unexpected voice, Banjo jerks upright, spins around and is blinded. 'Don't shine that thing in my eyes!' he growls.

Archie lowers the torch. He's sitting astride his bike just outside the fence. 'Sorry I took so long, Tully. Ussy's dad gave out prizes.'

'Did you get one?'

'Nah. Guess who got MVP.'

'Tamati?'

'Nils Telfer.'

'Seriously? He got fouled off more times last season than all the rest of us put together.'

'Ussy's dad changed him to guard. He's really good.'

Guard was Banjo's old position. He was never voted MVP. 'Did you bring food?' he asks.

'Heaps!' says Archie. He shines his torch on the bag of chaff. 'What's that?'

'Chaff. It's for Milly. But I can't get the darn thing open.'

Archie tips his bike against the fence and vaults over. He strokes Milly's cheek and says hello to her, then he stoops to examine the bag.

'Hold this,' he tells Banjo, passing him the torch.

Banjo directs the narrow beam not quite on his friend's face while Archie kneels and uses his teeth to gnaw through the nylon thread that stitches the bag closed. Then he unravels it in both directions until the top gapes open. The whole process takes less than 30 seconds.

'Anything else you'd like done?' he asks, sounding pleased with himself.

Banjo thinks about it. 'Have you got your phone?'

'Yes.'

'Can you ring my parents?'

13

Dude, We've Got Our Own House!

'Why can't *you* ring them?' asks Archie.

He and Banjo have dragged the bag of chaff along to the corner of the fence and propped it on an angle so it won't tip over. They stand side by side watching Milly eat. Archie holds the torch.

'Because they'll be mad at me,' Banjo answers.

'They'll be mad at me, too.'

'No they won't. They like you. And you aren't their son.'

Archie considers this. 'What will I say?' he asks finally.

'That I'm okay.'

'What if they ask where you are?'

That's the first thing they *will* ask. Banjo shrugs. 'Let's just forget about it for now,' he says. 'What food did you bring? I'm starving.'

Archie has done better this time – he's brought sausage rolls, doughnuts, party pies and six or seven slices of pizza. Everything is in a big Donut King bag and has come all the way from Usman's swinging from Archie's handlebars, so the food is a bit mushy and stuck together. But that doesn't matter – it's food. Banjo and Archie sit on the Viganos' back step eating in the dark. Archie is saving the torch batteries. Banjo eats more than his friend, who already had dinner at the basketball breakup, but even he is full before all the food is gone. They agree to save the rest for breakfast.

It's exciting to think that they'll be staying overnight in the deserted house. There are two compact sleeping bags stuffed into Archie's backpack. He tells Banjo the second one belongs to Usman's big sister, Jassi, who's spending part of her gap year staying with their grandparents in India ('Pakistan,' Banjo corrects him). Two cans of soft drink poke out of the little mesh pockets on the sides of the backpack. Archie checks with his torch and passes the lemonade to Banjo.

'See, I even remembered you don't like Coke.'

'It's Pepsi I don't like.'

'Sorry. Do you want to swap?'

'No, lemonade's fine. But thanks.'

They drink in the dark. Banjo can't see Milly, but he can hear her eating chaff over in the far corner of the yard. A mosquito buzzes in his ear. He tells Archie about the old man and the truck.

'You're a flukey sod, Tully!' Archie laughs when he's heard the full story.

'I'm glad you think so,' says Banjo.

'You are! You pull a crazy stunt like you did

today and then everyone you run into bends over backwards to help you.'

'Jabba wasn't exactly helpful.'

'He gave you a rope for Milly.'

Banjo sips his lemonade. 'He didn't *give* it to me.'

'But you *ended up* with it!' Archie argues. 'Like you ended up with a free bag of horse food and Ussy's sister's sleeping bag and dinner delivered right to your front door.'

'This is the back door.'

'Who died, Tully?'

'What?'

'You're acting like you're at a funeral.'

'Sorry. It's just . . .' Banjo lets his voice trail away. How can he explain what he's feeling? He doesn't really understand it himself.

He hears Archie take a big gulp of Coke. It's followed, a moment later, by a massive burp that goes rumbling out into the darkness. Banjo tries one, but Archie's was better.

'Can I use your phone?' he asks.

'Sure.' Archie taps in his password and hands it over. 'What are you going to tell them?'

'I'm not calling my parents, I'm calling Nan.'

'Tell her "hi" from me.'

Banjo squints down at the over-bright screen. He has just realised something. 'I don't know her number.'

'Is it in your phone?'

'Of course it is. But my battery's dead.'

'Check and make sure,' says Archie. 'There might be enough power left to open the phone book. Where is it?'

'In my backpack,' Banjo says. 'It's on the other side of you – can you grab it?'

They find Banjo's phone and try to switch it on. The flat battery icon comes up.

'What if we put my SIM card in your phone?' suggests Banjo.

'Are you with Optus?'

'Telstra.'

'Won't work then,' says Archie. 'My phone's locked on Optus.'

They finish their drinks in silence. Archie burps again, not so loudly this time, and tosses his empty can out into the yard.

'Litterbug,' Banjo says.

'I'll pick it up in the morning.'

Banjo tosses his can, too. 'Pick that up while you're at it.'

Archie laughs. They both laugh. Banjo tries another burp and it's the best one yet.

'Careful, you'll wake the neighbours,' jokes Archie.

Banjo wonders how close their nearest neighbours are. It would be really lonely here if he had only Milly for company. A bit creepy, too – he probably wouldn't sleep inside. 'Thanks for staying tonight, Arch.'

'Hey, I wouldn't miss this for the world,' says his friend. 'Dude, we've got our own house!'

They hear clinking noises out in the darkness. Archie switches on the torch. Milly has stopped eating and has come halfway back across the yard. She's bumping one of the empty soft drink cans along the ground with her mouth.

'She must be thirsty.' Banjo jumps up. 'Can I borrow your torch? I left her water bucket down near the clotheslines.'

Archie goes with him. They are careful to latch the gate behind them so Milly can't get out. Down at the clotheslines, Banjo shines the torch around, noting that the grass has been given a number one trim for as far as Jabba's rope let her reach. She has done all right today in the food department. But her water bucket has tipped over again. Banjo feels bad for letting her get so thirsty that she tried to drink from an empty soft drink can.

He isn't a good horse owner.

Back in the Viganos' laundry, Archie holds the torch while Banjo refills the bucket. He fills it all the way to the top this time, because he only has to carry it a few metres. Milly is waiting just outside, standing so close that Archie has to gently nudge her away with the screen door to get it open. While she's drinking, Banjo takes the torch and checks the chaff bag. There's still quite a lot left, but the top of the bag has collapsed inwards, making it hard to get at.

Banjo rolls the sides down so Milly will be able to snack on it during the night. He wonders if there will be any left by tomorrow morning. Probably – it's a big bag. Will he be able to take some of it with them tomorrow, perhaps in his backpack, or tied to the saddle somehow?

It's these thoughts that remind Banjo he has another job to do.

For the first time today, the drought is actually helpful. Because the ground has been so dry for so long, there's no undergrowth in the forest across the river where he left Milly's saddle and headgear. It only takes him and Archie a couple of minutes to find them. But on the way back, something bad happens.

Archie is leading the way with the torch. Banjo follows him, carrying the saddle. Suddenly, Archie veers to one side. Preoccupied with the phone call he will soon have to make to his parents, Banjo continues straight ahead. Something slaps him in the face. It's only a light slap, as if he has walked into a bunch of twigs. But then things get weird. The twigs seem to cling to his nose and eyelids and mouth.

And they are moving!

Banjo lets go of the saddle just as Archie swings the torch beam around and illuminates what's clinging to Banjo's face. It's a huge spider! He yelps, swats the horrible thing away and staggers backwards, almost losing his footing. Archie hoots with laughter.

'It's not funny!' cries Banjo, picking sticky threads of spiderweb off his face. 'You could have warned me!'

Archie is following the spider along the ground with his torch. 'It's only a golden orb,' he reports. 'They're harmless.' Then he starts laughing again. 'Dude, the look on your face!'

He's still going on about it as they walk up through the caravan park. Banjo wishes he would shut up. Archie can be a total pain sometimes.

But then he can surprise you. 'Hey, I just remembered something!' he says suddenly.

Banjo hopes it has nothing to do with spiders. 'What?'

They have arrived back at the house. Archie opens the gate and gently coaxes Milly to one side so Banjo can get through with the saddle. 'Remember when your pop got a new phone,' he says, 'and you and me helped him set it up?'

'Sure,' says Banjo. It was about two years ago, when Archie's family lived next door and Banjo's grandparents were still living on the farm. Archie was at Banjo's the day Nan and Pop came back from town with Pop's first ever mobile phone. 'What about it?' Banjo asks now.

'Your nan wrote down a list of names and numbers for us to put in the phone,' Archie reminds him. 'Her number was on the list and I noticed it was nearly the same as mine – I showed you, remember?'

Banjo doesn't remember. He carries the saddle up to the house and dumps it at the back door next to the rest of their gear. 'Was it, like, one number different or something?'

'Four,' says Archie, who is kneeling on the ground unzipping his backpack. 'The first six numbers were the same as mine, but last four were reversed.' His face lights up blue as he wakes his phone. He taps in a series of numbers, listens for a moment, then passes it to Banjo.

'It's ringing,' he says. 'Tell her hi from me.'

14

Seventh Heaven

'Hello?' says Nan's voice.

'Hi, Nan. It's me, Banjo.'

'Banjo! What a lovely surprise!'

It's a surprise for Banjo, too. Archie kind of sprung this on him. He hasn't planned what to say to Nan yet.

'Um . . . how are you and Pop?'

'Oh, much the same as usual,' she says cheerfully. 'We can't complain. What about you, dear? How is school?'

Obviously his parents haven't been in touch with her and Pop yet – she doesn't know that he wagged school today and hasn't gone home. 'Yeah, school's okay,' he answers.

'When are the holidays?'

'They start next week.'

'*Next* week?' Nan gasps. 'Heavens, we must have got our wires crossed! Pop and I were talking about it just this morning. We thought the holidays start the week *after* next. Have you got anything planned?'

'Not much.'

'How would you like to spend a week or so with Pop and me?'

There is nothing Banjo would like more; he wishes he was there right now.

'It's really lovely here at the moment, Banjo,' Nan continues. 'Everything is so green! And don't worry, there's lots of things you could do. Did you know Pop's got a boat now? He says to tell you the flatheads are biting at the moment.'

Banjo walks out onto the yard, holding the phone to his ear. He doesn't want Archie to hear the next part of their conversation.

'Nan, some stuff happened today . . .' he begins.

And the story comes pouring out of him. He wasn't intending to tell Nan so much, but just like when he got talking to that friendly council guy, Tuan Le, Banjo can't seem to stop himself. He doesn't tell her everything, though.

'Where are you now?' Nan asks when he's finished.

'I'm staying with a friend,' he answers – which is not a lie. 'Just for tonight. Nan, could you ring Mum and Dad, please, and tell them I'm okay? That I'm staying with a friend and not to worry about me.'

'Shouldn't you speak with them yourself?'

'I don't want to,' he admits. 'They'll make me tell them where I am, then they'll come and get me.'

Nan sighs. 'You will have to speak with them sooner or later, dear.'

Banjo has crossed the yard while they have been

talking. He stands very close to Milly, feeling the warmth of her on the side of his face. 'I know. But not yet. I'm still pretty mad at them, Nan.'

'All right, dear, I'll talk to them,' she promises. 'I'm not very happy with them myself, as a matter of fact. I wish I'd known they were thinking of selling Milly. She could have come here.'

This surprises Banjo. He has visited his grandparents twice since they moved — they live on a tiny block and most of the outside area is either paving or landscaped native gardens. 'Where would you keep her?' he asks.

Nan explains, 'Our neighbours over the back have got a big paddock that they don't seem to know what to do with. And we've finally had some rain here, did your dad tell you? There have been at least three good falls over the last six weeks. Everything has turned green! Yesterday I saw Graham, he's the husband, out there on his ride-on mower trying to get the grass under control. Milly would think it's seventh heaven.'

15

Happy Travels

A ringing noise drags Banjo out of a dream. It was a good dream. He was riding Milly across a lush, green paddock. The grass came halfway up her fetlocks. She was pausing here and there to graze (apparently it's okay for horses in dreams to eat with their headgear on). There was even a rainbow hanging in the sky. It's disappointing to leave all that behind and wake up in the dim, musty-smelling lounge room of the Viganos' old house. And to remember the drought.

The ringing noise has stopped. Banjo rolls over in his sleeping bag and sees Archie sitting up on the carpet next to him, half-out of his own sleeping bag, his phone pressed to his ear.

'Yes, Dad, it was great . . . ' he mumbles. 'Lots of food, yeah . . . Everyone . . . Is that today? . . . I totally forgot . . . I suppose so . . . But I've got my bike . . . Sure, they won't mind – I'll leave it in their shed . . . Okay, I'll be out the front.'

Archie ends the call and turns to Banjo. 'That was Dad. He's coming to pick me up.'

'Coming *here?*'

'No, to Usman's.' Archie kicks off his sleeping bag and begins scrabbling about for his clothes. 'I've got to get moving – he's going be there in twenty minutes.'

Banjo yawns. He's still half asleep. 'What time is it?'

'I don't know. Check on my phone.'

He finds the phone next to Archie's half-inside-out sleeping bag. 'What's the code?' he asks. Archie tells him and he taps it in. 'Ten past nine.'

'Poop!' says Archie. 'I *so* should have set the alarm! Can you see my other sneaker?'

Banjo points. 'Over by the door.'

'What's it doing over there?'

'You threw it at that cockroach, remember?'

Archie hops across the room on one foot, pulling his jeans on as he goes. 'I can't believe we got away with it.'

'Got away with what?' Banjo asks sleepily.

'Staying here last night. I thought we'd get sprung for sure. The guys aren't going to believe it.'

'You promised not to tell anyone.'

'It doesn't matter now,' Archie says. 'You're going home. Nobody will be looking for you.'

Banjo eases himself out of Usman's sister's sleeping bag and flips it to one side. His thigh muscles are sore from riding all the way from the farm yesterday. He stands up and arches his stiff back, hoping Milly has pulled up better than he has this morning.

'Where are you going?' asks Archie, lacing up his sneakers in the doorway.

Banjo steps over his legs. 'To check on Milly.'

It took him ages to get to sleep last night because he was worrying about her out there in the yard. Did they latch the gate properly? What if something spooked her in the dark and she injured herself on the fence? Or tried to jump over it? He was worried about other things, too. Would he be able to find enough food for her? For both of them? What if they got lost? . . . No wonder he's so tired.

Milly is fine. She's over in the far corner of the yard with her nose in the chaff bag. Banjo hobbles across the hard, flinty earth in bare feet. He's wearing what he slept in – just his rumpled school shirt and jocks – but who will see?

'Hey Mills,' he says. She swings her big head around and allows him to stroke her muzzle. Then she snorts, blowing dust in his face and returns to her breakfast.

'I talked to Nan last night,' Banjo tells her. 'How would you like to go and visit her and Pop?'

Behind him, the laundry door rattles open and Archie comes outside, fully dressed and wearing his backpack. 'I left you the rest of those doughnuts and stuff,' he says. 'They're near the fireplace with your other gear.'

'Thanks.'

'Can you look after the other sleeping bag? I

couldn't find the bag it goes in and there wasn't time to stuff around looking for it. If Dad gets to Ussy's before I do, things could get complicated.'

'Why is he picking you up?' Banjo asks.

'We're going to my cousins' over in Wentworth,' Archie explains as he gets his bicycle from around the side of the house. 'It's my uncle's birthday — I forgot all about it.'

Banjo opens the gate and Archie high-fives him on the way through. Banjo almost tells him what he's planning, but stops himself when he remembers his friend's problem with keeping secrets.

'See you, Arch,' is all he says.

'Happy travels, dude!' Archie calls over his shoulder as he scoots his bike into motion and goes pedalling off through the caravan park with his helmet swinging from the handlebars.

Banjo stands by the open gate, his friend's parting words repeating in his head: *Happy travels, dude!* Archie has no idea.

Back in the house, Banjo finds the grease-stained Donut King bag balanced tidily on his backpack near the fireplace. He opens it and separates most of a squashed sausage roll from a sticky mass of doughnuts and pizza. The pastry has green icing and hundreds and thousands stuck to it. Sweet and sour, Banjo thinks as he takes his first bite, but there's no one to share the joke with. Suddenly, he feels sad — he and Archie were going to have this weird breakfast together. On the plus side, Banjo now has enough food for more than one meal. He can eat some for breakfast and save the rest for lunch and maybe even for dinner tonight.

He also has a sleeping bag. How lucky is that! He was reluctant to ask Archie if he could hang onto it because his friend would have wondered why. He finds the drawstring bag it goes in scrunched up next to his hoodie and jeans. Archie didn't look very hard. Kneeling to roll up the sleeping bag, he discovers Archie's phone lying on the carpet underneath. Yikes!

Banjo hurries outside with the phone, hoping Archie has remembered and come back for it. But there's no sign of him. He wakes the phone and makes a call.

Usman picks up straight away. 'Hey Archie, what's up?'

Banjo can hear several boys' voices talking and laughing in the background; it makes him feel lonely. 'This isn't Archie,' he says, 'it's Banjo.'

'But . . . that's Archie's phone.'

'He left it behind. Is he there yet?'

'He just left,' Usman replies. 'His parents came and got him. They're going to Whitecliffs or somewhere.'

'Wentworth. It's his uncle's birthday.' Banjo picks something out of his teeth – it's a tiny white pellet, the last of the now not nearly hundreds and thousands (Archie would like that joke, too). 'I was hoping he'd still be there. Did he get to your place before his parents?'

'Only just,' says Usman. 'Mum saw him riding in. He said he'd been to the shops.'

Banjo laughs. Archie can talk his way out of any situation. It should be him running away on a horse, not Banjo. 'Can you do me a favour, Uz? Can you come to the caravan park and pick up his phone?'

'I've got to clean up here,' says Usman. 'Take it home with you, Banjo. It's not like Archie can't live without his phone for a couple of days.'

What about a couple of *weeks*? Banjo is tempted to ask.

Back in the lounge room, he opens his backpack and slips Archie's phone in next to his own in the narrow inner pocket. He puts everything else into the main compartment, including the hoodie – it's going to get hot later. Then he changes his mind, takes it out again, removes his school shirt and pulls the hoodie on with nothing underneath. They won't be looking for someone wearing a blue hoodie and jeans. Unless Archie talks about it. It's a shame he's so bad at keeping secrets – Banjo would have liked to talk to someone about what he's planning. He almost told Usman.

On the other hand, he hasn't fully made up his mind yet.

Before putting on his borrowed jeans, Banjo applies a crisscross of band-aids to the insides of both his knees to prevent further rubbing.

'Thanks for having us, Viganos!' he calls back into the empty house as he lets himself out through the laundry door, clicking it locked behind him.

There is still some chaff left in the bag. It's too bulky to fit in his backpack, but Milly will need food. Banjo tips half its contents onto the dusty ground, then folds the top of the bag down and kneels on it to make it more compact. By rearranging everything in his backpack, he manages to fit the three-quarters-empty chaff bag in too. It's heavy, though. He has to use the Viganos' back fence to climb aboard Milly. Then he rides slowly down into the wide empty riverbed. He jinks the reins and Milly pauses obediently. This is crunch time. There are two options: either they can turn right and go back to their drought-stricken farm, or they can turn left and go somewhere that's lovely and green.

The voice of reason tells Banjo that the second option is a stupid idea. But Nan's voice from last night reminds him, *Milly could have come here.*

Banjo clucks his tongue and gently nudges Milly with his knee.

They turn left.

16

Knight in Shiny Armour

They stop for lunch in the stippled shade of a big rivergum. Banjo unsaddles Milly and gives her the remaining chaff. The sun is high overhead. It must be about midday. He checks Archie's phone but there's no signal. They're in the middle of nowhere. He hasn't seen any livestock, nor any other signs of agriculture, for at least two hours. There was an old orchard earlier on, but it looked abandoned.

Banjo eats standing up. He's not used to sitting in the saddle for extended periods. At least his knees haven't been rubbing today, thanks to the jeans and the band-aids. Milly seems to be holding up okay. She finishes the chaff and wanders down to drink from one of a string of tiny pools that still occur at intervals along the riverbed. Chewing on a sticky mouthful of doughnut, Banjo wonders how far they have come since leaving the caravan park.

Earlier, when he had a signal, he brought up Google Maps on Archie's phone and plotted his route to Nan and Pop's. He and Milly will follow the riverbed for the first 82 kilometres – that way they can avoid roads, where people will see them. But the river veers to the south just past Nullambine, leaving them no choice but to use roads from that point. They will still have another 750 kilometres ahead of them. It's better not to think about it.

Banjo takes another bite from the doughnut. There's a cheesy taste of pizza, too. It was nice of Archie to bring all this food. And the clothes. And the band-aids. And Usman's sister's sleeping bag. But what is Banjo going to do about Archie's phone?

If he turned back now, he could probably arrive home before dark. His parents will be expecting him. Nan promised to call and tell them he's going home today.

It's still not too late to turn back.

Banjo finishes the doughnut and washes it down with a tiny sip of water. Then he carefully plugs the neck of the bottle with a broken-off piece of coat hanger rod he found in one of the Viganos' wardrobes. He has to make his water last. And his food. Saving what's left from Archie's basketball breakup, Banjo stows his lunchbox away for later.

A few kilometres further on, they come to a bridge where a road crosses the river. It's their third bridge today. The first two were high enough to ride under, but this one is too low. Pausing for a moment to listen for traffic, Banjo urges Milly up the sloping clay embankment onto the road. *Uh oh!* At the other end of the bridge, about 60 metres away, a blue four-wheel drive with a caravan attached is parked at the side of the road. A grey-haired man kneels in the gravel next to one of the wheels. A woman, also with grey hair, stands between the caravan and the safety railing, looking in Banjo and Milly's direction. Now the man sees them, too. Scrambling awkwardly to his feet, he waves both arms above his head and calls out to Banjo, but the distance is too great for his words to carry.

Banjo was hoping to cross the highway without being noticed. Word might have got around about a missing boy and a horse. Pretending to misinterpret the man's gesticulations, he waves cheerfully back.

But the man calls again and this time one of the words is unmistakable: 'Help!'

Banjo can't ignore that. Reluctantly, he pulls Milly around and starts towards them. They look like 'grey nomads' – retirees from some faraway city making their once in a lifetime trip around Australia and seeing how the country people live. So why not give them a show? thinks Banjo. For the first time today, he allows Milly to canter. Her iron-shod hooves beat out an impressive drum solo on the bitumen as they clatter down the middle of the bridge. *Yee ha!*

He reins Milly to a stop just in front of the four-wheel drive. It's a late model Nissan Patrol with blue and white WA registration plates. The front nearside wheel has been lifted up on a jack. A fold-out toolkit lies open on the gravel.

'Puncture?' he asks.

The man nods and looks Banjo up and down. 'You look like a strong young fellow. Would you be so kind as to help me get this last wheel nut loose?'

Swinging down from the saddle, Banjo leads Milly past the caravan and hitches her to the safety barrier. He removes his backpack and helmet and returns to the Nissan. 'Let's have a try,' he says.

The man hands him an L-shaped wrench. 'The bottom nut has rather got the better of me. Whoever did it up must have been on steroids.'

Banjo has watched his father change wheels several times. He knows how it's done. Fitting the socket end of the wrench to the stuck wheel nut, he grips the long end with both hands, spreads his feet wide and heaves upwards. The nut resists for a moment, then comes loose with a satisfying metal-on-metal squeal.

'Bravo!' The woman claps her hands. 'We were about to call the NRMA when you came along.'

Banjo wipes his sweaty palms on his jeans. 'You would have been lucky to get through. There's next to no mobile reception out here.'

Together, he and the woman's husband change the wheel. Banjo does most of the work. Yesterday everyone was helping him, today he's giving back.

When the job is finished and everything is packed away, the wife returns from the caravan with two glasses of water. She hands one to her husband and the other to Banjo. 'You men have earned this.'

It feels good to be called a man. Banjo thanks her and drains his glass in one long, gulping swallow.

'Good heavens, you *were* thirsty!' She takes his empty glass. 'I'll get you some more.'

Banjo drinks his second glass more slowly. He and the grey nomads stand next to their caravan, sipping their water and brushing away flies. The road at this point is several metres higher than the surrounding countryside, which is huge and flat and dry. Halfway to the horizon, a tiny ute crosses a wide brown paddock, leading a herd of cattle. A cloud of red dust hangs over them. The ute stops and the driver gets out and climbs onto the tray.

'What's he doing?' asks the grey nomad husband.

'Feeding them.'

They watch the farmer throwing clumps of what must be hay to the hungry cattle.

'Poor cows,' says the grey nomad wife.

Poor *farmer*, thinks Banjo.

'We can't believe how dry it is over here,' she continues.

Her husband agrees. 'We crossed the Nullarbor a few months ago and it was greener than this.'

Banjo sips his water. 'We've been in drought for almost as long as I can remember.'

'Are you from a farm?' asks the wife.

'Yes. But we've had to sell all our cattle.' Banjo doesn't like to think about it. 'There's no grass anymore. It's too expensive to keep buying hay for them. We can't even afford to have a horse, now.'

The grey nomads look at Milly and Banjo is annoyed with himself for shooting his mouth off like he did twice yesterday. Next, he'll be telling them that he's running away to Nan's place.

A semitrailer saves him from saying anything else he might regret later. It comes thundering across the bridge from the other end, rocking the caravan and mussing up everyone's hair as it gusts past. Milly whinnies in alarm and almost pulls her reins free of the safety barrier. Banjo hurries back to quieten her.

The woman follows him, taking his empty glass so his hands are free. 'Those truck drivers don't give you much leeway, do they?'

'He could have slowed down a bit, that's for sure,' agrees Banjo, stroking Milly.

Another vehicle comes speeding across the bridge – a car this time. It goes flashing past only a few metres from where they stand.

'I guess this isn't the safest place to park,' says the grey nomad husband, who has joined them. He looks at his wife. 'We should get moving, Glenys, before someone snaps off one of our side mirrors.'

Banjo nods. 'I've got to go, too.'

'Are you going far, love?' asks Glenys.

'No.'

She looks at his backpack, lying on its side near the safety barrier where he dropped it earlier. There's a damp patch in the gravel where his stubby hangs almost upside down in one of the side pockets. Banjo quickly rescues it, but it's empty.

'My water bottle,' he explains to Glenys, in case she thinks he's been drinking beer. 'The cork wasn't very good.

'May I?' She takes the stubby from his hand and disappears into the caravan. Banjo imagines her in there sniffing it, to check if he was lying about its contents.

He only told her one lie and that wasn't it.

Glenys returns with an unopened bottle of spring water and hands it to him. 'The lid on this one is better.'

'Thank you,' he says. It feels lovely and cool.

'You're more than welcome, love. I don't know what Bill and I would have done if you hadn't come along.'

'Someone else would have stopped if I didn't.'

Her husband, Bill, shakes Banjo's hand. 'Thanks for your help, champ. You're a lifesaver.'

'Our knight in shiny armour,' Glenys says.

They say their goodbyes and the grey nomads climb into their Nissan. Banjo puts on his backpack and clips up his helmet.

'Wait a minute!' calls Glenys.

She comes hurrying back from the Nissan and walks around behind him. He feels a slight tug on his backpack and hears the zipper open.

'What are you doing?'

'It's just a little something to help you on your way, love,' she says, zipping the backpack closed again.

As soon as Glenys and Bill have driven off, Banjo removes his backpack and looks in the rear compartment. Jammed down between the two phones is a wad of twenty dollar notes. He counts them: one, two, three, four, five. $100!

Something to help you on your way.

He wonders if Glenys was somehow onto him. Did she suspect he was running away?

But I'm not running away, Banjo thinks, I'm running *to*.

17

Being a Kid Sucks

Banjo was wrong. He told the grey nomads there would probably be no phone signal here, but when he checks Archie's phone there are three bars. He brings up his friend's call history and dials the number he rang at 7:34 pm yesterday.

'Hello?'

'Hi, Nan. It's me again.'

'Banjo!' She sounds almost as surprised as she did last night. 'Where on earth are you? I was just talking to your father.'

Now it's Banjo's turn to be surprised. And worried, too. 'I thought you were going to call him last night.'

'I did,' replies Nan. 'This time he phoned me. Where are you? You should be home by now. They're expecting you.'

A car is coming. Banjo moves closer to Milly and catches hold of her bridle. He should have led her away from the road before making this call. The car slows and moves over into the other lane as it crosses the bridge towards them. They must be country people. Banjo gives them a thank you wave and they wave back.

'The thing is, Nan,' he continues once the car has passed, 'I'm not going home, I'm coming to your place.'

'I beg your pardon?'

He repeats it.

'I don't understand.' Nan sounds confused. 'When are you coming?'

'Now.' Banjo rubs his thumb under the snaffle strap where it runs down Milly's cheek. 'We're on our way. I'm riding Milly.'

There's a short silence. 'Now let me get this straight, Banjo. You intend to ride Milly all the way here?'

'That's right. It's just over 800 kilometres, but I figure if we can do, like, 100 or maybe even 120 kilometres every . . .'

Nan isn't listening. 'I hope this is some kind of joke,' she interrupts.

How can she think it's a joke? 'Last night you said you wanted me to visit,' Banjo reminds her. 'And you said you wished you knew that Dad and Mum were going to sell Milly, because there's an empty block behind your place where she can live.'

'I know I said that.' Nan sounds sad and apologetic. 'Sometimes people say things on the spur of the moment – things they don't mean literally. I shouldn't have given you the impression that I wanted Milly here. Good heavens, Pop and I can't possibly take on the responsibility of looking after a horse at our age.'

Banjo sucks on his lower lip. It feels sunburned. 'But you said you were cross that they sold her.'

'I was,' admits Nan. 'I still am, as a matter of fact. They shouldn't have done it without telling you — that was wrong. But, Banjo, you have to look at it from their point of view — they can no longer afford to keep her. And the people who bought her own a riding school down in Gippsland; it's lovely there, they never have droughts and Milly will be well looked after.'

Banjo touches his head against Milly's cheek. *He* can look after her.

'Banjo? Are you still there?'

'Still here.'

'You have to go home,' Nan says firmly. 'And I want you to phone your parents straight after this and let them know where you are. They're very worried.'

His parents are the last people Banjo wants to talk to right now. 'Why don't *you* phone them?' he says, ending the call.

It's hopeless. Even Nan is on his parents' side. Nobody cares what *he* thinks.

Being a kid sucks.

18

Tree Cemetery

It's only after he and Milly begin their long journey home that Banjo comes to realise how ridiculous his plan was. They would never have got to Nan and Pop's. Even with the money Glenys gave him, it's not like he could stop and buy food and water whenever they needed it – towns might be 100 kilometres or more apart. And where would they have stayed at night?

Late in the afternoon, he and Milly reach the abandoned orchard they passed on their outward journey. He needs a break. They both do. It's a relief to swing down from the saddle. Banjo frees himself from the sweaty clutch of his backpack and drops his helmet on top of it. Removing Milly's bridle, he watches her walk down towards a little, reedy pool in the centre of the riverbed. Her ears are pricked forward, her tail is held high. She seems none the worse for the many kilometres she has carried him over the past day and a half. He feels a sudden rush of affection for her. And then he remembers that she's been sold.

Life is not fair sometimes.

Carrying the bottle of water Glenys gave him – it's mostly empty now – Banjo wanders up to look at the orchard. It's all spiky sticks and knobby trunks. But right in the middle, a single tree clings to life. Little yellow baubles decorate its otherwise bare branches. Banjo finished the last of his food a couple of hours ago – there wasn't much left anyway – and he's been hungry all afternoon. Part of a split Cootamundra wattle has fallen across the boundary fence and he uses it as a wobbly bridge. His thigh muscles are sore. The fruit turn out to be pears, but they are tiny – hardly bigger than walnuts. Banjo twists one free of its sinewy stalk and takes a tentative bite. It nearly breaks his teeth. But inside its tough skin, the flesh is surprisingly sweet. Banjo eats three or four, then he begins collecting a few more for later.

'This is private property!'

The voice startles him. Banjo turns around, concealing his hands behind his back.

A girl in a white T-shirt and blue shorts comes marching through the stick trees towards him. Her sneakers kick up angry little puffs of red dust. 'Those are our . . . ' she begins, but the sentence remains unfinished.

They stare at each other, wide-eyed.

Banjo recovers first. 'Hi.'

'What are you doing here?' asks the Year 10 girl who called him 'the boy from Snowy River' yesterday.

Sheepishly, he reveals what's in his hands. 'Stealing your pears, I guess.'

He is relieved when she smiles. 'Apart from that,' she says. 'I mean, how did you get here?'

'On my horse.'

'It's Milly, isn't it?' The girl looks around. 'Where is she?'

Banjo is impressed that she remembers the name. 'Down in the river.' He points, but the dip of the riverbed hides Milly from view. 'We're just taking a break,' he explains.

'And stealing our pears.'

'Yeah, that too. Do you want them back?'

'No, you're welcome to them. I came down to get some for the chooks, but you can have as many as you like.' She pulls a face. 'They look pretty awful, though.'

'They are quite sweet actually.' He offers her one.

'I'm not that desperate.'

Banjo grins self-consciously – he's been eating chook food. 'I was collecting a few for Milly.'

'She'll want more than that.' The girl begins picking pears off the tree and dropping them into a little pouch she makes by lifting up the bottom of her T-shirt. Banjo makes a similar pouch with the front of his hoodie and goes around the other side to fill it.

'Are you in some kind of trouble, Banjo?' the girl asks through the branches.

'No.' He stretches up to pick the highest pear on

his side of the tree. 'Not really. How do you know my name?'

'Everyone knows your name after that stunt you pulled yesterday.'

'What's yours?'

'Mai,' she tells him. 'Mai Le. You met my father yesterday, too. At River Bend Park?'

'No way! The guy watering the Canoe Tree was your dad?'

'He's a bit of a conservation nut.' Mai smiles at Banjo through the pear tree. 'We all are, in my family.'

It's not long before both their pouches are full.

'Let's go and see if Milly likes stolen pears as much as you do,' Mai says playfully.

Banjo's sunburned face feels hot. 'Only the ones I picked before you arrived are stolen.'

'You sound like a lawyer,' she teases.

'It's better than being a thief.'

They both laugh.

Mai leads the way down through the tree cemetery. Banjo waits while she crosses the wattle tree bridge ahead of him. When it's his turn to cross, he sees her notice his school shoes.

'I guess I am in a bit of trouble,' he admits.

Banjo shows Mai how to hold her hand flat so Milly can pick the tiny fruit off her palm with her big, soft muzzle. Mai flinches the first couple of times, but soon she gains confidence. Watching her feeding his horse, Banjo tells her a long, true story.

By the time he's finished, all the pears are gone and Mai is studying him with a half-worried, half-amused expression. 'I can't believe those caravan people paid you a hundred dollars just for changing a flat tyre.'

'That's not why they gave it to me,' Banjo says. He's been thinking about it all afternoon. 'It was because we got talking about the drought and I more or less told them that my parents are going broke.' As soon as the words are out, he regrets saying them. What's with him lately – shooting his mouth off to everyone he meets?

And there's something shameful in admitting your family has no money.

Milly begins nudging Mai in the chest, pushing her backwards. Mai looks nervous. She might be in Year 10, but she's smaller than most of the girls in Banjo's year. And Milly is a very big horse. Banjo steps between them and begins rubbing the corners of Milly's mouth, which is something she likes almost as much as eating. It's like stroking a cat. 'There aren't any left, Mills,' he tells her.

To Mai, he says, 'Sorry about that. She just wanted more pears.'

'Then let's go and get her some.'

'She's probably had enough. Any more and she might get colic.'

'Then take some with you to eat on the way home,' suggests Mai.

Banjo smiles. She's nice. 'Okay. Thanks.'

They return to the orchard. This time Banjo brings his backpack. He follows Mai around the tree, holding it open while she picks the rest of the stunted fruit and drops them in. It isn't long before they are back where they started. Now the tree is as bare and as dead-looking as its neighbours.

While Banjo kneels to zip his backpack closed, Mai looks around as if noticing the state of the orchard for the first time. 'Before the drought,' she says in a sad, dreamy voice, 'we used to get enough pears from these trees to fill six or seven bins. Proper sized pears, not munted little things like these. My aunts and uncles used to come up from Melbourne to help pick them.'

'How big were the bins?' asks Banjo.

'Like this.' Mai spreads her arms. 'And probably just as tall.'

'That's a lot of pears.'

She nods. 'It used to take them a whole weekend. Six adults. Now you and I can do it in five minutes.'

Banjo puts on his backpack and Mai accompanies him back down to the fence. She watches him climb across the fallen tree. Milly is waiting on the other side, hoping for more pears. He ruffles her mane. 'You've had enough for now, greedy girl.'

While Banjo goes to collect her bit and bridle, Mai leans over the fence and strokes Milly's nose – they seem to be friends again.

'What time will you get home, Banjo?' she calls.

'We won't get there tonight.' He checks the position of the sun. 'We'll probably stay at the caravan park again. How far are we from town here?'

'Fifteen kilometres.'

That's by road. Following the riverbed, it could be further. He studies the angle of the sun as he walks back towards Mai's boundary fence. 'We should make it to town before dark.'

Mai is silent for a moment. 'Why don't you stay here?'

'Here?' he says, clipping on his helmet.

'Yes. Here. At my place.' She points behind her but all he can see are dead pear trees. 'You could sleep in the pickers' quarters and we could bring Milly into this paddock. There's a gate further along.'

She seems to have it all worked out.

'Would it be okay with your parents?' asks Banjo.

'Of course!' Mai smiles brightly. 'My mother would love to meet you, too. Do you like Vietnamese food?'

19

If There Wasn't a Drought

Banjo has never tried Vietnamese food, but if he is ever asked that question again he will be able to answer with a yes. Mai's mother is a great cook. They start with homemade spring rolls and a choice of three dipping sauces. One sauce is fiery hot and Mai warns Banjo to try only the tiniest bit to begin with. He takes her advice, then drinks a whole glass of water and sticks to the other two sauces after that. The main course is a tasty chicken and cashew stir-fry, filled with so many weird vegetables that every mouthful is a surprise; but they are nice surprises, except for the deadly little peppers that he quickly learns to push to the edge of his plate. Banjo has a second serving when Mrs Le offers it.

Mr Le – Tuan – smiles at him across the table. 'Make sure you leave room for dessert, Banjo.'

Mrs Le brings the dessert to the table in a large, earthenware bowl. Steam rises out of it. With a ladle, she fills four smaller bowls and Tuan passes them around. Banjo studies what's in his bowl. It resembles lumpy green soup. For dessert? Everyone else is eating, so Banjo dips his spoon in and, as he did with the fiery sauce that came with the spring rolls, has a tiny taste.

Mai is watching him. 'What do you think?'

'It's nice,' he says. But it's the weirdest dessert he has ever tasted – sort of vegetably and sweet at the same time. 'What is it?'

'Mung bean pudding,' she says.

'Are they your own mung beans?'

'Yes. Mum and I picked them this morning.'

Mai's mother sees Banjo glance at her and she smiles. He returns her smile. She's friendly but she doesn't talk much. 'This is great, Mrs Le,' he says. 'I've never tasted mung beans before.'

Until today, he had not even heard of them. When Tuan showed him around their property earlier this evening, he told Banjo how their family are experimenting with other crops now that their orchards have failed. Last year they pulled out 140 dead fruit trees from their front block to make room for two hectares of mung beans. Thanks mostly to bore water, the spring planting was quite successful. But when they resowed in February and their underground water supply finally dried up, the total mung bean harvest was only enough to feed the family.

Tuan was a full-time orchardist until two years ago. Now he goes to town five days a week and works for the council. It's mostly Mrs Le who looks after what's left of their orchard and gardens. Tuan and Mai help on weekends. But Banjo senses that the drought is slowly getting the better of them.

After dinner, he offers to help with the washing up, but Mrs Le shoos him out of the kitchen. 'You are our guest, Banjo. Go and sit down.'

Back in the dining room, Tuan asks, 'Would you like to use the phone, Banjo?'

He and his wife are very polite. They have not asked Banjo a single question about what happened since yesterday morning or what he intends to do tomorrow. Mai must have filled them in on some of the details earlier – while he was having a shower out in the pickers' hut, where he's staying tonight – because her parents have acted as if dusty, hungry, sunburned boys on horses turn up at their orchard every day. Banjo knows what Tuan is really saying: *Perhaps you should phone your parents.*

'That's okay, Mr Le, I've got my own phone.' In fact, he has two. They are both out in the pickers' hut – his is plugged into a charger Mai found for him, Archie's is still in his backpack. There's good coverage here – he checked on Archie's phone – but Banjo is in no hurry to call his parents. He knows he should, though. They were expecting him home this afternoon. No doubt Nan called them after he hung up on her. He still feels bad about that.

'I might go and make a call now,' he says.

Mai follows him to the door and hands him a

torch. 'You might need this.'

'Thanks.'

'And here's an old shirt one of my uncles left here,' she adds, thrusting a bundle of black and red chequered cloth into his arms. 'I thought you might be more comfortable in something nice and fresh. Can you find your way in the dark?'

Banjo nods. The pickers' hut is about 50 metres from the main house, but he's been back and forth several times already. 'I'll be okay with this torch.'

'Come back when you're finished. We can watch a movie.'

The pickers' hut is like a tiny, single bedroom holiday house. It even has bunk beds. Banjo stands in the bathroom inspecting his clothes in the spotty mirror. They seem clean enough. Then he sniffs under one of the sleeves of the faded blue hoodie he's been wearing all day. *Wowsers!* No wonder Mai suggested he get changed. He hopes her parents didn't notice, too. Banjo imagines seemingly shy Mrs Le drawing her daughter aside as Mai goes to fetch the torch and whispering, *See if you can persuade him to put on this nice clean shirt Uncle Henry left here.*

How will it feel to go back there in a few minutes, wearing Uncle Henry's shirt like an admission of what everyone was too polite to mention? He could avoid the embarrassment by wearing his school shirt instead. But when Banjo digs it out of his backpack, he discovers it's just as pongy as the hoodie. What to wear when he goes back to Mai's house is a problem he can deal with later. There's something more important to do first.

'Hi Dad, it's me.'

'Are you all right?'

'Yes.'

'Where are you? We were expecting you home this afternoon.'

'I know. I'm sorry. It was further than I thought when I was talking to Nan. I only got halfway home before it started getting dark.'

'Where are you now? We'll come and get you.'

'No, Dad, it's okay. I'm staying at a friend's place. I'll come home in the morning.'

'Who is the fr –?'

'Bye, Dad, see you tomorrow.' End call.

Banjo is glad that's over. It would have been so much easier to talk to his mother, but there's no mobile coverage at home so he had to call the landline and speak to whoever picked up first. Banjo can't believe he hung up on his father. That's twice in one day that he's done that to a family member. But this time he had no choice – his father would have become angry and loud and Banjo would have caved in and told him where he was. Then, half an hour later, Mr Tully would be standing at Mai's front door, telling her parents he's here to pick up his runaway son.

That would be even more embarrassing than the unmentioned BO.

Banjo turns off Archie's phone before his father can call back. His skin feels clammy. It's lucky he didn't put on Uncle Henry's shirt before making the phone call. Stripping off the rest of his clothes, he has his second shower of the evening, this time paying attention only to his armpits.

He gets dressed in the bedroom. The shirt fits quite well. But it's an old man's shirt – Banjo wouldn't be seen dead in it in public.

Back in the bathroom, he uses the bar of soap from the shower to wash his smelly hoodie in the handbasin. Then he washes his school shirt, too. At least he can show his parents that he's been looking after himself. And looking after Milly.

He checks on her before returning to the house. They've put her in the 'River Block', which is what Mai's family call the old pear orchard. There's an open-sided packing shed that makes a nice stable. Milly stands in the shadows over in the far corner, either asleep or half asleep. Banjo doesn't go over there in case the torchlight disturbs her. Masking the beam with his fingers, he checks the old iron bathtub they're using as a drinking trough. It's still about one quarter full. There's lots of hay left, too – *actual* hay, not straw. Shortly after Banjo and Milly arrived, Tuan drove off in his little Suzuki Jimny and returned with a hay bale that he got from one of their neighbours. When Banjo offered to pay for it, Tuan smiled and said it was a gift from him to Milly.

Mai and her parents are such great people. Banjo

wishes he could stay here for more than just one night. It's the school holidays, after all. If there wasn't a drought, he could pick fruit or do other work around the orchard every day – he wouldn't expect to be paid – and spend his nights in the pickers' hut. But if there wasn't a drought, he wouldn't have come here in the first place. He wouldn't have met Mai because she's in the year above him at school. And his parents wouldn't have sold Milly.

But there *is* a drought, these things *have* happened and Banjo has to go home tomorrow.

20

Go and Tell Them

'You didn't have to knock,' Mai says, opening the front door for him. 'Come in, Banjo. That shirt looks nice on you.'

They join her parents in the lounge room. Mr and Mrs Le sit in mismatched armchairs watching the news. They greet Banjo but don't comment on the shirt. Mai leads him to a three-seater cane couch and they sit at either end.

'We'll watch a movie after this,' she says quietly. 'Dad always likes to see the weather forecast.'

'He's hoping for rain,' Mrs Le comments.

Banjo isn't sure if she's serious or making a joke, but Tuan gives him a wink.

The news is almost over. Just before the daily sports roundup, a final item comes on about something called a 'Climate Emergency Summit' in Canberra next week. Banjo isn't paying much attention – he's thinking of telling them about the rain gauge he left in Matilda's great-grandfather's truck – but Mai and her parents are staring so intently at the screen that it would be rude to interrupt.

When the report is over, Mai seems angry. 'Nothing will come of it! In the end, the decision makers will say it's people in other countries who are wrecking the climate and nothing we do here in Australia can make any difference.'

Banjo keeps his eyes on the TV, where a line of male sprinters crouch at their starting blocks.

'What do you think, Banjo?' Mrs Le asks, just as the starter's gun fires. 'If you had the chance, what would you say to those decision makers in Canberra?'

Banjo is taken by surprise. He hasn't really thought much about climate change, except that it's obviously bad. Lots of people even think it's causing the drought, but others – like Nan and Pop, who have lived here forever – say there have always been bad droughts in Australia. Mai and her parents are waiting for him to say something, though, and Banjo doesn't want to seem like someone who doesn't care about environmental issues.

'I'd tell them to think about their kids,' he says, hoping that's a good answer. 'It's our generation – Mai's and mine – that will have to deal with what they're letting happen to the planet.'

They watch *The Hobbit*. Mai borrowed the DVD from the public library. Banjo saw it at the cinema when it first came out, but he doesn't tell her. It's a long movie. Her parents watch for a while, then say goodnight and go to bed.

As soon as they are alone, Mai pauses the DVD and turns to Banjo. 'I've had this idea.'

He waits for her to continue but she doesn't. 'So what is it?' he asks.

'You'll probably think it's silly.'

'*Is* it silly?'

Suddenly, Mai springs up off the couch. 'Would you like a drink? I made some lemonade this morning.'

'That sounds good.'

She disappears into the kitchen and returns a short time later with two glasses trembling brimful with pale, cloudy liquid. Handing one to Banjo, she sits back down at her end of the couch. But she doesn't resume the movie.

Banjo sips his lemonade. 'This is really nice.'

'Thanks. We've got so many lemons this year.'

'I didn't see any citrus trees when your dad gave me the tour,' he says.

'There's only one.' Mai stares into her glass. 'It's just behind our herb garden. We keep it and the herbs alive with recycled water from buckets we take into the shower with us.'

Banjo feels guilty. There was a red plastic bucket in the shower in the pickers' hut, but he had been too preoccupied to think of using it. 'So when are you going to tell me your idea?' he asks.

Mai fiddles with the TV remote. 'There are two ideas, actually, but they're sort of connected.'

'I promise not to say they're silly,' says Banjo.

Instead of telling him her two ideas, Mai asks a question: 'On a scale of one to ten, how badly do you want to keep Milly?'

'Ten.'

'All right, I think I know how you can do it.' Mai sets her still-full glass on the coffee table in front of them and looks Banjo in the eye. 'Have you heard of crowdfunding?'

'Is that when someone starts a website to raise money for a charity?' he asks.

'Not just for charity,' she says. 'It can be for almost any good reason. Do you know Amber Galloway from our school? She holds the Australian record for the Under-16s high jump.'

Banjo nods. 'I thought it was the state record.'

'She broke the state record first. But last December she flew to the national championships in Cairns and set a new Australian record.'

'How high did she jump?'

'I don't remember.' A little frown pinches up the skin between Mai's eyebrows. 'That isn't the point, Banjo. Amber wouldn't have gone to Cairns at all without crowdfunding. Her mother runs that little gift shop next to the Post Office and it's not doing so well lately.'

'Is that Amber's mum?' asks Banjo. 'She gave me a discount last year when I didn't have enough for a Mother's Day present.'

'I hope it wasn't a *big* discount,' Mai grumbles.

'It was only 50 cents, I think.'

'Sorry, I shouldn't have got grumpy with you,' she apologises. 'It's not you I'm mad at, it's what we're doing to the planet. But I'll get to that in a minute.' Mai dips a finger into her glass and licks it. 'I was telling you about Amber going to Cairns. When Ms Cartwright at school heard they couldn't afford the airfares, she helped Amber set up a site called *Help 15-Year-Old State Champion Compete for National Title* and they raised six thousand dollars.'

'You're kidding!' Banjo gasps. He sees she isn't. 'But there's a difference between flying a girl who's already a state champion to a national athletics competition and raising money for a kid no one's ever heard of who just wants to keep his horse.'

'There *is* a difference,' she agrees. 'So here's my second idea, Banjo. You know that thing you said to Mum about how the decision makers in Canberra should think about their kids?'

He nods warily.

Mai's face lights up. 'Well, why don't you go and tell them!'

21

Eco Warrior

It's very late by the time Banjo returns to the pickers' hut. He and Mai did watch the rest of the movie, but neither paid much attention to Bilbo Baggins's adventures. Mostly they talked and planned. Mai did most of the planning – she's good at that. Her idea isn't totally silly, but Banjo has misgivings about the role he would be expected to play in it.

It's the starring role.

But unlike Bilbo Baggins, who has a band of loyal friends to help him overcome the many obstacles that confront him on his journey, Banjo and Milly would be on their own.

Mai assured him they wouldn't be totally on their own. They'd have lots of online supporters. She has already dreamed up a name for the site: *Sponsor 15-Year-Old Eco Warrior's Epic Ride to Save Farm*.

'That's a bit of a stretch, isn't it?' Banjo said when she first told him.

'How is it a stretch?' asked Mai. 'Milly is part of the farm. If you raised enough money to keep her, that'd be one less expense your parents would have to worry about. So you'd be helping them, as well as keeping Milly.'

'I actually meant the Eco Warrior bit,' he said.

'Oh.' Mai's dark eyes sparkled. 'I'm quite proud of that. Don't you think it sounds punchier than what Ms Cartwright wrote about Amber?'

'But Amber actually *was* State Champion,' Banjo pointed out. 'I'm not an Eco Warrior.'

Mai leaned towards him, placed her fingertips lightly on his arm and spoke earnestly: 'Banjo, if you did this, you *would* be an Eco Warrior — you'd be helping save the planet!'

The whole thing is certainly doable. Canberra is 42 kilometres closer than his grandparents' place — Mai showed him on her phone — and he and Milly would have twelve days to complete the journey. But Banjo's reason for doing it *wouldn't* be to save the planet. What he said to Mai's mother about the decision makers listening to their kids was just something he overheard on the car radio a couple of weeks ago when his mother was driving him to Venturers.

And then there's the whole question of getting the okay from his parents. He would have to tell them what he's doing. If he doesn't go home tomorrow, they will definitely come looking for him. They might even report him missing: *Police have mounted a statewide search for a 15-year-old boy and a horse.*

'Sleep on it,' Mai suggested two minutes ago, as

they whispered good night at her front door. 'Make up your mind in the morning.'

Banjo unplugs his phone. It's fully charged now. There are dozens of texts, missed calls and voice messages. Most of the calls and voice messages are from the landline at home. He doesn't bother reading them or going to voicemail, he simply turns the phone off. He's a coward.

Sorry Mum and Dad, he thinks, I'll call you in the morning.

Before going to bed, Banjo goes into the bathroom to check the hoodie and shirt he left hanging over the shower rail to dry. They are still quite wet. Taking them outside, he drapes them over the verandah railing. There's a slight breeze, they might be dry by morning. Banjo is about to go back inside when he sees a little round light wobbling towards him from the direction of Mai's house.

Her voice comes out of the darkness, 'I was worried you might be in bed already.'

'No, I'm still up,' he says unnecessarily. 'What's happening?'

She joins him on the verandah and gives him a brown paper bag. 'I brought you some toothpaste and a toothbrush. Don't worry, they're new.'

Banjo doesn't look in the bag. When he calls his parents in the morning, he'll tell them he's old enough — and responsible enough — to take care of himself. 'What we were talking about before,' he says to Mai, 'I think I'll do it.'

'Really? Are you sure?'

'Totally.' It's only as the word leaves his lips, that Banjo realises he has made up his mind – he and Milly are going to Canberra! 'But I'm not any kind of Eco Warrior,' he adds.

'We'll see,' says Mai, shining her torch on his wet washing. 'These will never dry out here. I'll take them up to the house and hang them in the airing cupboard.'

Banjo doesn't know what an airing cupboard is, but he has no doubt that it will dry his clothes if Mai says it will. She's a great organiser. 'Thanks for going to all this trouble,' he says.

'You're no trouble at all, Banjo.' Carrying his wet hoodie and shirt, she steps lightly down the stairs. 'Nite nite.'

'Nite, Mai.'

As he watches her disappear into the darkness, Mai's words echo in his head, *You're no trouble at all*.

But Banjo can't remember a time when he's been in *more* trouble.

22

Day One

Banjo wakes on a bare mattress, staring up at a spotty white ceiling that's so close he could touch it. It takes him a few moments to remember where he is. He chose the unmade top bunk even though the one below him is fully made up with blankets, fresh sheets and a matching pillowcase. It seemed wasteful to sleep there for just one night. How much water does it take to wash two sheets and a pillowcase? He slept in his sleeping bag instead and used his rolled-up jeans as a pillow. It was good practice for what's to come.

Today is day one, Banjo tells himself as he drops feet first onto the creaky floorboards between the bunk beds. *Owww!* His legs are even stiffer today than yesterday.

He switches on his phone to check the time. 10:04 am. Yikes! Still, it's Sunday and people often sleep in – especially if they stayed up till nearly midnight planning crazy horse rides to Canberra. It *does* seem a bit crazy this morning, Banjo thinks, but too late now. He hopes Mai slept in, too. She told him to come up to the house for breakfast, but she didn't say what time. He turns the phone off and quickly gets dressed.

When he opens the outside door, Banjo finds the clothes he washed last night neatly folded in a hessian shopping bag that's been left on the doormat. He takes them inside. His school shirt has been ironed! And he notices a faint, eucalyptus-y smell when he pulls the hoodie down over his head, which makes him suspect that Mai gave his clothes a second wash before putting them in the airing cupboard. As he sets out towards the house, Banjo smiles to himself and plans what he will say to her about wasting water.

It's a conversation for later, though. Halfway to the house, Banjo sees Mai's father driving across from the work sheds on an ancient grey tractor. When Tuan notices him, he brings the tractor around in a wide semi-circle and pulls up beside him.

'Good morning, Banjo. Did you sleep well?'

'Yes thanks, Mr Le.'

'That's good. Go and have breakfast.' Tuan nods in the direction of the house. 'Mai's not there, but my wife is expecting you.'

'Where is Mai?' asks Banjo.

'She went off with some friends,' her father says. 'She said to tell you she won't be long and not to leave until she gets back.'

Up at the house, Mrs Le leads Banjo through to the dining room. There are two boxes of cereal, a bowl and a spoon set out at the place where he sat last night. 'I will get you some milk for the Weet-Bix,' she says. 'Would you like orange juice or a cup of tea?'

'Orange juice would be great thanks, Mrs Le.'

Banjo feels embarrassed sitting alone at the table. He wonders when Mai had breakfast. He's surprised she went out with friends instead of waking him. Tuan said she won't be long, but it's more than 800 kilometres to Canberra and he wants to get moving as soon as possible.

Mai still isn't back by the time he's finished breakfast. It must be 10:30 by now. He should ring his parents, but he'll just pop down and see Milly first. She isn't in the packing shed. He can't see her anywhere and begins to get worried. Then he hears the tractor start up. Guided by the noise, Banjo walks down through the old orchard and finds Milly watching Mai's father. He has hooked one end of a heavy chain around the trunk of a dead pear tree and attached the other end to the rear of the tractor. Tuan revs the engine, smoke billows from the rusty exhaust pipe and the chain trembles; then, almost in slow motion, the tree surrenders, dragging a tangled nest of roots up out of the bone-dry earth as it collapses into the dust. *Whump!*

Tuan shuts off the tractor's engine, climbs down and walks over to Banjo and Milly. He rubs the side of his jaw, leaving a blood-red smear of dirt where the itch was. 'Ten down, thirty-six to go,' he says ruefully.

Only now does Banjo notice that a whole row of pear trees have been ripped out of the ground like the one he just witnessed. He strokes Milly's big, warm neck and struggles to find something to say. Two days ago, he watched this same man lovingly watering the Canoe Tree.

'Are you going to grow mung beans here?' he asks finally.

The former orchardist shakes his head. 'There's a new strain of olive tree that's supposed to be quite drought-tolerant; I'm thinking of giving them a try.'

Banjo hears a door bang shut, followed by the double toot of a horn as a car drives away. He turns to look, but all he can see are skeletal pear trees.

'That'll be Mai's friends dropping her off,' Tuan says.

Wearing red jeans and a white, long-sleeved top, Mai is crossing the driveway from the pickers' hut as Banjo walks up from the River Block.

'I'm over here!' he calls.

Mai veers in his direction. There's a mischievous sparkle in her eyes, as if she's harbouring a secret. 'Have you been up long, Banjo?'

'About an hour. Where did you go?'

'Me and Amber went shopping.' She isn't carrying anything, though.

'Who drove you?' he asks.

'Amber's big sister came with us.' Her smile disappears. 'I hope it's all right, Banjo – I put some things in your room. Come and have a look.'

When they reach the pickers' hut, she turns and puts a wait-a-moment hand on his arm. 'Before we go in, Banjo, I want you to know that this doesn't make any difference. I'm not trying to put pressure on you. If you've changed your mind, that's totally okay.'

'I haven't changed my mind,' he says.

Her face relaxes. 'Cool!'

There are three large shopping bags on the table. The side of one has flopped down and Banjo can see the blue lids of several bottles of spring water poking out. On the floor is a big yellow and black duffel bag with its price label still attached.

Mai opens one of the shopping bags. 'This one's just food,' she says, lifting out a shrink-wrapped cube of Two Minute Noodles. 'There's all sorts here. We got mostly dehydrated stuff, so it's not too heavy for you and Milly to carry. There's lots of noodles and these ready-to-go pasta meals – you just have add hot water. Do you like porridge?'

Banjo nods. For a moment he's lost for words. He wouldn't have thought of any of this. Yesterday morning – was it only yesterday? – he set out for Nan and Pop's with no provisions apart from the leftovers from Archie's basketball party and a badly-stoppered bottle of water. He ran out of everything by early afternoon. And he still had ten or twelve days of travel ahead of him. It's lucky he turned back.

And it's so lucky he met Mai!

While Banjo is having these thoughts, more and more food items are being laid out on the table: cereal, powdered milk, muesli bars, hot chocolate, biscuits, dried fruit, little tins of sardines.

'Who paid for all this?' he asks.

'We did,' Mai says distractedly. She's unloading the second bag now. This one doesn't contain food. Out come matches, soap, sunscreen, batteries, a little torch, a red plastic cup-plate-and-bowl set, a tea towel, a scourer, a mini pack of tissues and she's still not finished! 'One roll or two?' Mai asks, holding up a twin pack of toilet paper.

Banjo shrugs. 'Maybe both?'

She pulls out the next item. 'Tamara – that's Amber's sister – thought these might be the right size,' she says, not meeting his eyes.

It's a six-pack of underpants. The label says *Medium*.

'They'll be good,' he says, blushing.

Mai skips the third bag – 'It's all bottles of water,' she tells him and lifts the duffel bag up onto the table. There is barely room for it now with everything else stacked there. 'We had to wait around until ten for Cliff to open so we could get this stuff,' she explains. 'That's why we took so long.'

She means *Cliff's Hardware and Camping*. Banjo is

surprised it opens at all on Sundays. He sees there's something inside the duffel bag. Mai opens the long zip and pulls out a green and black chequered shirt.

'We got you this because it's got long sleeves and you'll be out in the sun a lot,' she says, holding it up. 'Do you like the colour?'

'It's okay.'

'Amber said it's like high country stockmen wear – I told her how I called you the boy from Snowy River,' she explains as she reaches into the duffel bag again. 'And look, here's a hat. It's not exactly an Akubra, but it's got this adjustable chin-strap so it shouldn't blow off. Try it on.'

Banjo obediently puts on the hat. It's dark grey and made of stiffened cloth. Mai studies him and nods her approval. Several more items come out of the duffel bag: a miniature camping stove, complete with two cartons of fuel tablets; a small square saucepan with a nifty hinged top that opens out to become a bowl with a handle; an aluminium knife-fork-and-spoon set; a can-opener; a First Aid kit; and, last of all, a little tent. She's thought of everything.

Mai should have been a scout!

'All this stuff must have cost you guys heaps,' he says. 'How much do I owe you?'

'Nothing.' She smiles. 'Consider this the first donation towards your epic ride to save the planet.'

It isn't to save the planet, though, it's to save Milly. But Banjo doesn't correct her.

23

Intrepid

Everything fits into the duffel bag. But they have trouble arranging the six 1.5 litre bottles of water so the load sits squarely behind Milly's saddle. The big, heavy bottles pull the bag out of shape and threaten to tip it off balance. Banjo and Mai unpack and repack it several times, moving things around to redistribute the weight, but they can't fix the problem.

'I give up!' Banjo sighs after their third or fourth attempt. 'I'll have to leave a couple behind.'

Mai shakes her head. 'No way. That water is the most important thing you're taking with you, Banjo. And it's not just for you, it's for Milly too. You won't be following the river all the way to Canberra.'

They are in the packing shed. Milly has wandered off to nibble at what's left of the hay bale. Banjo saddled her five minutes ago so they could work out where to place the duffel bag, but he hasn't put on her headgear yet. 'We'll be passing lots of towns and farms,' he says. 'There'll be dams.'

'You can't rely on it,' warns Mai. 'A lot of dams are empty now. And people have left their farms.'

Banjo knows she's right. This whole thing is about water. Or *lack* of water, to be more accurate. 'I'll have to use my backpack then.'

He was hoping to leave it behind. It's up in the pickers' hut, along with his school clothes, Uncle Henry's shirt and Archie's phone. Mai promised to drop the phone off at Archie's next time she's in town. Banjo gave her the address.

'I've got an idea,' she says. 'Stay here, I'll be back in a minute.'

She returns with two of the sturdy hessian shopping bags she brought back from her trip to town. Banjo watches as she threads the four carry-straps through each other in a complicated knot.

'Tah dah!' Mai says proudly, holding up what she's made. 'Saddle bags.'

It's ingenious. The connected straps fit between Milly's saddle and her saddle blanket, allowing the bags to rest snugly against her flanks. With three bottles on each side, they are perfectly balanced. The duffel bag is lighter now and its ends are supported by the makeshift saddle bags. Banjo uses the orange twine from Milly's hay bale to secure everything to the four metal eyelets on the rear of the saddle. Finally, he attaches her headgear and puts on his own new hat. They are good to go.

Trying not to worry about what he's taking on, Banjo leads his laden horse out into the bright sunshine. Mai walks beside him, matching his steps as they make their way between the rows of dead pear trees. Neither of them speaks.

They pass the silent tractor. Banjo is relieved that Tuan isn't there. Mai hasn't told her parents what he's planning to do – they think he's going home. How would he explain his loaded-up horse if they saw him?

Mai surveys what her father has done to the lower part of the orchard. It looks like a tornado has gone through. 'Poor Dad,' she says softly.

Banjo is close enough to hear. 'He reckons he's going to plant olive trees,' he tells her. 'A new kind that do okay in droughts.'

'I know.' Mai picks up a wizened branch and snaps it in two. 'But even they won't make it if it doesn't rain some time.'

They both look up at the boring blue sky.

'Do you think we *can* do anything about climate change?' he asks.

'Of course we can,' says Mai. '*We have to!*'

They arrive at the boundary fence. She opens the little gate and Banjo leads Milly through. The river looks even drier than it did yesterday. It takes two attempts to get into the saddle – the duffel bag gets in the way of Banjo's leg the first time he tries to swing it over. He will have to get used to that.

Is he really going to Canberra?

'Smile!' Mai stands back with her phone raised, taking a photo of him and Milly. She lowers it, checks the screen and frowns. 'Your face is too shaded.'

Banjo takes his hat off.

'No, you need to be wearing that,' she says. 'This is for the website. Just push it back a bit and tilt your chin up . . . that's good . . . and now we'll try one without the smile.'

'You said to smile.'

'It's better if you don't, I think. I want you to look intrepid.'

'Like an Eco Warrior?' he jokes.

'Exactly,' she replies seriously. Mai seems to believe he *can* make a difference. All Banjo wants is to keep his horse.

'When will you put the site up?' he asks.

'Tomorrow.' She's peering at her phone, shading the screen with her hand. 'I'm going over to Amber's in the morning. Tamara's going to help us. I'll send you the link when it's done.'

Banjo doesn't think he has ever spoken to Amber Galloway and he has never laid eyes on her big sister; yet they are both helping him.

'Are the photos okay?' he asks.

Mai nods. 'There are a couple of good ones.'

'Do I look intrepid?'

'Totally.'

Now there's nothing left to say except a muddled exchange of awkward thank-yous and goodbyes and promises to call tonight and to look after Milly and to be careful.

Banjo doesn't look back until he and Milly have reached the first bend in the river. Mai is still standing exactly where he last saw her. She waves and Banjo raises his hat in his best imitation of a high country cattleman's salute.

Then he nudges Milly with his knees and they gallop intrepidly away.

24

Home Sweet Home

Galloping was a mistake. But Banjo doesn't realise it until many hours later, when he's setting up camp.

He's found a good spot next to a dense stand of sheoaks, about 60 metres from the riverbed. It's a little half-clearing, protected on three sides by trees. The open side faces the river. He can see Milly foraging among the reeds. There's an almost-dried-up pool surrounded not only by reeds but also several varieties of native grass. That's why he chose this site. Finding food and water for Milly is going to be one of Banjo's greatest challenges over the next dozen or so days. But right now, he's thinking about his own needs. Two muesli bars, a couple of cream biscuits and a little packet of dried sultanas are all he has eaten since breakfast; he's starving! First, though, there's a tent to put up. It will be dark soon.

It's while he is unloading the duffel bag that Banjo discovers why galloping was a mistake. Everything is dusted with fine, white dust. There's a hole in the milk powder box. One of the little camp stove's sharp, metal corners must have stabbed through the cardboard when he galloped off around the corner from Mai's farm.

'That'll teach you for showing off,' Banjo mutters to himself. He won't tell Mai about this when he phones her later.

Taking everything out of the duffel bag, he raises one end and shakes the spilled milk powder down to the low end. Then he painstakingly scoops it up with his new spoon and tips it back in through the hole in the box. He patches the hole with band-aids. It's a nice piece of improvisation; Banjo feels pleased with himself. Maybe he *will* tell Mai!

The tent is a simple A-frame design similar to the ones they use in Venturers, only it's smaller and the fabric is much lighter. It's a cinch to put up. Banjo brings Milly's saddle over and uses one of the stirrups to hammer the pegs into the hard, dusty earth. Then he unrolls his sleeping bag and arranges it inside. Home sweet home, he thinks. And wishes he was there.

For his first official Eco Warrior dinner, Banjo combines the contents of two packs of instant noodles and heats them on the little stove. When they are boiling, he adds some tinned sardines and stirs everything together with a stick. It's an okay meal, but no way would it get him onto *MasterChef*. Banjo eats straight out of the little aluminium cooking pan, then licks it clean.

The remains of the fuel tablet are still sputtering

away in the lower section of the stove. It seems a shame to waste it. Using the licked-clean pan, Banjo heats some water and makes a cup of lumpy hot chocolate. The first sip burns his tongue. While he waits for it to cool, he fetches his mobile phone and turns it on for the first time since leaving Mai's.

Uh-oh! There's no signal. He should have called his parents first thing this morning and told them what's going on. They'll be going mental. But there's nothing he can do about it now. Night is falling. Collecting Milly's rope, Banjo walks down to the river to find his horse.

By the time he has returned to the campsite and tethered Milly to one of the sheoaks, it's fully dark. He thinks about making a small campfire to push the shadows back, but decides not to risk it. He's surrounded by trees and the ground is carpeted with their tinder-dry needles. Last summer's bushfire season was one of the worst on record. Mai was talking about it last night; she's really worried about climate change.

She's the one who should be going to Canberra.

Sitting on Milly's spread-out saddle blanket with his new torch balanced on one knee, Banjo sips his hot chocolate and eats one of the cream biscuits from the opened packet. Then he eats a second one. Soon, all the biscuits are gone. Stupid! he thinks. There were only three packets to begin with. He will have to be more disciplined from now on, limit himself to a small number of biscuits each day – two with lunch, two in the evening – otherwise he'll run out before he's even a quarter of the way to Canberra.

He wonders how far he and Milly have come today. Further than yesterday, anyway – they passed the bridge where he met Glenys and Bill several hours ago. But without mobile coverage and access to Google Maps, it's impossible to know where they are now. Banjo feels totally isolated, totally cut off from every other human on the planet.

It's the loneliest feeling.

Finishing his hot chocolate, Banjo tries the phone again. Nothing. He stands up and walks around, lifting the phone above his head, tilting it this way and that, but still there's no signal. Before turning the phone off to save the battery, Banjo checks the time. The display says 7:22 pm. It's much too early to go to bed, but what else is there to do?

Sleep is a long time coming. The sleeping bag is warm and comfortable, Banjo's body is super tired after all those hours in the saddle, but his brain won't shut down. He keeps hearing noises outside the tent. Is that Milly shuffling about out there, or something else – a possum, bush rats, mice? Before going to bed, Banjo put all his non-tinned food into the hessian panniers and used a piece of baling twine to hang them from a tree branch so animals couldn't get at them. It's something he learned in Scouts. But did he hang it high enough? What if a fox or a dingo comes along? They can jump quite high. A fox probably wouldn't come into camp with Milly here, but a dingo might. Would a dingo spook her?

Banjo rolls over onto his other side. He wonders what his parents are doing right now. It was totally stupid not to phone them this morning while he had the chance. They'll be worried sick. They are probably driving around looking for him right now. He wouldn't be surprised if they have called the police.

He is in so much trouble!

With all this on his mind, it's no wonder Banjo can't get to sleep . . .

Then he opens his eyes and it's light outside.

25

I Totally Agree

There's a town ahead. The tops of two huge white grain silos rise above the feathery brown treetops. To the right of them is a church steeple.

Banjo doesn't need Google Maps to confirm his whereabouts. He can't remember the names of all the towns along the route he and Mai planned on Saturday night, but Nullambine was the first of them. It's an important milestone. This is where he and Milly have to leave the river. From now on they'll be travelling on roads.

Reaching Nullambine is important in another way, too. There will be a phone signal here. Finally, Banjo can call his parents.

He is not looking forward to it.

He stops and dismounts. It feels like lunchtime. He'll eat lunch first, then he'll make the phone call.

'Stop putting it off,' he growls at himself. 'Call them *now*!'

Banjo unloads Milly and heaves the saddle and blanket off her wide, sweaty back. He removes her bit and bridle, freeing her to go and forage in the riverbed. He hopes she finds clean water this time. They stopped about an hour ago, but there were swirly rainbow patterns on the water's surface and Milly wouldn't drink it. Banjo had to fill his little saucepan with bottled water and let her drink from that. The pan was much too small and she spilled more than she drank. They used up one-and-a-half bottles of their precious water that way. Now there are only two bottles left. But that no longer matters – Banjo can get more water in Nullambine. He opens one of the two remaining bottles and takes a long, satisfying drink. Down among the reeds, Milly seems to be drinking too. It's all good. Or it would be, he thinks, if he didn't have to make this phone call.

There are five bars of signal. Banjo stares at the screen. He has eighteen missed calls and messages. Most are from his parents, but two are from Mai. He opens the first one. *Hi Banjo . . .*

That's all he gets to read, because suddenly the screen flashes and the phone is ringing. It's his mother. Here goes, he thinks.

'Hi Mum.'

'Banjo! Thank heavens! Where are you?'

He hesitates. His mother has called him from her mobile phone, which means she isn't at home because there's no signal there. She must be in town. It's only a half hour's drive from Big River to Nullambine. He doesn't want her to come looking for him.

'I'm not sure exactly,' he says, turning away from

the silos. 'But I'm okay, Mum. Milly's with me and it's all good.' His mother starts to say something, but Banjo keeps talking. He has been rehearsing this all morning and he needs to say it quickly.

'I'm sorry for not phoning yesterday and telling you what's going on. I knew you and Dad would be worried. I tried calling a couple of times this morning, but there was no signal till just now. But don't worry, Mum, me and Milly are both okay. We won't be home for a few days though – we're doing something important.'

'I know,' she says calmly. 'Your friend Mylie told me all about your Canberra expedition.'

Banjo doesn't correct her about the name – he's too surprised and confused. 'How . . . ?' he stammers. 'Who . . . ? I mean, where did you get her number?'

'I didn't have her number,' replies his mother. 'I called her by accident. Apparently you left Archie's phone at her place and she picked up when I tried calling him last night.'

'Why did you call Archie?'

'Banjo, you've been missing for three days,' she reminds him. 'Your dad and I have been frantic. We've been phoning everyone.'

Did you call the police? he wonders. But he doesn't ask that. 'I'm sorry for making you and Dad worried.'

'Well, yes, you could have called us sooner and saved us a lot of worry.'

'I'm really sorry, Mum.'

'And so you should be,' she scolds. 'But never mind all that, we've found you now.'

But they haven't found him yet – he hasn't told her where he is. Even so, Banjo knows it's over. Of course they won't let him go to Canberra, he was never going to get their permission. He's almost relieved.

'It wasn't just about Milly,' he says, thinking about some of the things he's learned over the last couple of days. 'All of us should do something about climate change, Mum. Before it's too late.'

'I totally agree,' she says.

26

Greetings From Mars

Banjo and his mother make a deal. He has to stay in touch. He has to phone home at least once a day to tell his parents where he is (if he knows), how he is and how Milly is. If there's no signal, he has to stop and try again every two hours until there *is* signal. He has to promise to look after himself and to take good care of Milly; to make sure they both eat properly and drink lots of water; to re-apply sunscreen three or four times a day; to wash regularly; to brush his teeth; to avoid taking risks; and to be super careful on the roads. And if something goes wrong: if he or Milly gets sick, or if they run out of food or water, or if Banjo simply changes his mind and wants to turn back, all he has to do is call his parents and they'll come with the horse trailer and bring them both home.

If he agrees to all that – and, of course, he does – Banjo has his parents' permission to ride to Canberra.

When the call is over, he pumps his fist and nearly drops the phone because his hand is so sweaty. He can hardly believe it. He has caused his parents a whole lot of stress and worry, but after speaking to Mai they calmed down a bit. Mai must have made a really good impression! Apparently Banjo's dad was harder to convince than his mother. But after Mum reminded him that at the age of seventeen (not much older than Banjo) she spent six months backpacking in Asia and nothing bad happened to her, he finally agreed. Best of all, not once during Banjo's whole conversation with his mother did she mention selling Milly.

He decides to celebrate. There's a Macca's in Nullambine. Their bus stopped here on the way back from the Year 8 Camp last year. It's just past the big roundabout on the other side of town. He and Milly will be riding right past it. So far, Banjo has not spent a single cent of the one hundred dollars that Glenys, the grey nomad, gave him. He can afford a Big Mac. And it will be so much nicer than muesli bars, dried fruit and his lunchtime limit of two biscuits.

Banjo allows Milly another twenty minutes to finish her own lunch – she has found more than just water down there among the reeds. It gives him the opportunity to read Mai's text messages.

The first one is short: *Hi Banjo, hope you and Milly covered lots of k's today. I guess there's no signal cos you haven't called. Sweet dreams x Mai.* He stares at the *x* for a few moments, but it's probably just a girl thing.

The second message was sent 24 minutes after the first one. It's long – Banjo has to scroll down and down to read it all. Mai explains how she heard Archie's phone ringing in his schoolbag and the caller ID said *Tully*. She knew that was Banjo's second name, so she answered and *Guess what, it was your mother!!!* Banjo's mother was calling to see if Archie knew where Banjo was. She and Mai ended up having a long, long talk. Banjo's mother sounded so nice and she was so worried about Banjo that Mai simply *had* to tell her what was going on. At the end of the message, Mai apologises for shooting her mouth off and hopes Banjo isn't mad at her. She finishes with a sad face emoji and another of those *x*'s.

Banjo isn't mad at her. She has done him a huge favour by telling his mother about Canberra. He isn't sure he could have sold the idea to his parents, but Mai can be pretty persuasive. She talked *him* into it! On the phone just now, his mother said what a lovely, sensible girl Mylie was and how she was looking forward to meeting her one day.

Finally, Banjo had had to set her right about the name. 'It's Mai Le, Mum – first name Mai, second name Le. Her family's from Vietnam. Her mother is an excellent cook.'

Banjo isn't sure why he mentioned Mrs Le's cooking. Perhaps because he's hungry?

There is nowhere to tether a horse at McDonald's. The carpark is small and uncomfortably close to the road. It's a busy highway. When an eighteen-wheeler truck swooshes past, Milly's ears go back and she tosses her head. She's still spooked from nearly being run down by Lynnie and Carol on Friday. Banjo dismounts and strokes her neck, talking softly into her ear. He has no option but to lead her on foot through the drive-through lane. Luckily, they are not busy. There is only one car ahead of them, a blue SUV with an interested kelpie watching Milly through the rear window. Banjo waits until it moves forward, then he orders a Big Mac Meal with extra fries. The intercom voice tells him to drive round to the first window.

'Woah! A horse!' gasps the boy at the window. His nametag says *Ben* and he looks about Banjo's age. He also looks worried. 'Um, I think this is only for cars.'

'I have to do it this way,' Banjo explains, 'because there's nowhere to leave horses out the front.'

'What's the problem?' asks someone behind Ben.

'There's, like, a guy here with a horse.'

A woman peers over Ben's shoulder. She must be the supervisor. 'You can't bring a horse through here!' she growls.

'I just want to buy lunch,' says Banjo.

'I'm sorry, sir.' She shakes her head. 'It's only for people in cars.'

He can't believe it. 'We're not hurting anybody. Look, I've got her fully under control.'

But there are some things nobody can control. Banjo hears a series of dull slapping sounds on the concrete behind him. Uh oh! He turns reluctantly to look and, sure enough, Milly has just dropped a big pile of poo in the middle of the drive-through lane.

'Sorry,' he says to the very cross looking woman in the window. 'Have you got a shovel or something? Or a big plastic bag? I'll clean it up.'

'Just get your horse off the property!' she snaps, while Ben, sitting in front of her, covers his mouth and tries hard not to laugh.

There's a car waiting to come through behind them, so Banjo has to lead Milly forward. As they pass the next window, a girl beckons to him from inside.

'Here, take your order,' she says in a half-whisper.

'But I didn't pay for it,' Banjo half-whispers back.

'It's your lucky day then.' The girl is smiling. 'I had it all ready for you. A Big Mac Meal with extra fries? Take it! We'll just have to throw it away otherwise.'

Banjo eats his free meal on the steps of the ancient bluestone church with the tall steeple he spotted from the river. It's a weekday, so nobody is here to tell him that horses aren't allowed in the churchyard. Milly has moved into the shade of a tall palm tree leaning over the wall from the school playground next door. It's a church school and there's a narrow gateway connecting the two properties. Banjo sips his Coke and looks at the rusty gate. It's the school holidays – the kids' toilets will be locked, but there will be drinking fountains. He'll be able to refill his empty water bottles and give Milly a top-up before they set out on the next leg of their journey.

The friendly girl at McDonald's was right — it *is* his lucky day.

Banjo's good luck continues all afternoon. The route he and Mai plotted on Google Maps avoids big, busy highways wherever possible. There's a little side road just outside Nullambine with a faded sign that says *Harvest 98*. That's the next town he and Milly have to pass through. It's an arrow-straight road with a wide, dusty verge, ideal for a horse and rider. Banjo keeps Milly to a steady rising trot. She doesn't seem tired, but he doesn't want to push her — or to push his good luck — so occasionally he eases her back to a walk for a kilometre or two.

Riding along the roadside is easier than following the riverbed and they seem to be making good time. They see only three vehicles — two utes and a dusty four-wheel drive — all of them travelling in the other direction. The drivers all wave and Banjo waves back. They must wonder where he's going on his loaded-up horse. Twice, he and Milly stop for a drink. She is getting better at drinking from the cooking pan, but it's a messy business and quite wasteful. Already they have used nearly half their water. Banjo will have to buy a bucket in Harvest tomorrow; they won't get there today. According to Google Maps, from Nullambine to Harvest is 98 kilometres, which is much too far for Milly to cover in a single afternoon. (B's horse, in Mr Turbot's maths quiz, was obviously galloping. Banjo still wonders if Archie and Usman were telling the truth about that.)

The next time they stop for a drink, Banjo checks his phone to see how far they have come, but – no surprise – there's no signal. The time says 5:15 pm. He will have to find somewhere to camp soon, however nothing around here even remotely resembles a suitable campsite. All he can see is 360 degrees of flat, empty horizon. There are no trees, no hills, no buildings, no dams. And not a hint of green. This is the wheatbelt, it must have all been planted out in crops not too long ago, but now it looks like a desert. So depressing!

But there's an upside: because livestock have never been farmed here, there are no fences. Banjo can set up camp wherever he wants. He chooses a spot about 150 metres from the road – close enough to see it, but far enough away for Milly not to be spooked by passing traffic.

The ground here is carved into a repeating pattern of grooves and ridges, evidence that a seeder or a plough has turned it over at some point. There are lines of crunchy, brown stubble where a crop has failed. Banjo stamps out a flat area and puts up his tent. He gives Milly some water, wipes the pan clean, then sets about cooking dinner. Tonight, he'll have one of the pasta meals.

The sunset is spectacular. Half the western sky lights up as if it's on fire. While he's waiting for the pasta water to boil, Banjo powers up his phone and positions himself in front of his tent. Milly is nibbling at the stubble in the background. He lines everything up and takes a selfie. The photo looks awesome – like they're camped on another planet – but one detail is wrong. Banjo fetches his hat from the tent and poses again. Perfect!

The signal isn't strong enough to make a phone call, but sometimes text messages get through. Banjo types: *Hi Mai. Greetings from Mars. Banjo :)*

He presses Send.

27

Just a Kid

They reach Harvest late the following morning. A sign on the outskirts of town says *Level 6 Water Restrictions Now in Place*. Banjo didn't know they went that high. It makes him even more aware of his nagging thirst. He and Milly have no water left. They shared the last bottle for breakfast. Banjo's portion went into his muesli. Carelessly, he tipped in too much milk powder, turning the cereal into a gluey mush. It might have satisfied his hunger, but he really needed something to wash it down afterwards. That was nearly four hours ago. Only two cars have gone past today and both drivers misunderstood when Banjo waved at them to stop so he could ask for water – they simply waved back and drove on.

He dismounts outside the first house they come to. There's a two-tone brown SUV in the carport, with kids' booster seats in the back. Plastic toys lie scattered across the dusty yard and a trampoline takes up one corner. A mother will take pity on him. He ties Milly's reins to the front fence and knocks on the door.

The woman is nice. She brings him a glass of water and a bucket to fill for Milly. There's a tap near the trampoline. Two small children crowd in the doorway watching. The girl looks about four and the boy is a toddler. They both want to see the horse. Their mother leads them out onto the driveway, holding the boy's hand. Everyone watches Milly drink.

'Big doggie!' says the boy.

'It's a horse,' his sister corrects him.

Banjo asks the woman if it's okay to fill his water bottles and she says, 'Of course.' The little girl helps him – she's in charge of the lids. She lines them up along the brick garden edge and carefully screws each one on when the bottles are full. Banjo tightens them afterwards.

'Is there somewhere in town that sells farm supplies?' he asks the mother.

'*Tarrant and Sons*.' She points down the road. 'It's just before the roundabout, you can't miss it.'

She and her children stand out on the dusty footpath waving as he and Milly ride away. He's only known them for fifteen minutes, but they seem like old friends. Banjo misses his parents.

The slow *clop-clop-clop* of Milly's hoofbeats echoes off the shop fronts in Harvest's main street. Banjo has never been here before. The streets are unusually wide, allowing room for vehicles as large as farm trucks to reverse-park with their tail lights overhanging the deep gutters. Most of the parking spaces are empty. Several vacant shop windows display signs saying *Closed* or *For Rent*. They remind Banjo of what happened to *Burgess Plants and Gardens* back in Big River. Only *Tarrant and Sons*, the big agriculture and hardware store on the corner near the roundabout, seems unaffected by the drought. Two utes, an old station wagon and a crookedly-parked Toyota Landcruiser with a trailer are parked outside.

A faded sign with an arrow says: *Loading Yard at Rear of Building*. Banjo rides around the back, finds the entrance and dismounts. He's a bit worried about bringing Milly into the yard after what happened at McDonald's yesterday, but what else can he do?

A man in shorts and a khaki shirt with *Tarrant and Sons* embroidered on the pocket is stacking rolls of fencing wire. He straightens up when he sees Banjo and Milly. 'What can I do for you, pilgrim?' he asks.

Banjo smiles nervously. 'Can I buy some food for my horse?'

'How much do you need?'

After hearing Banjo's story, the man disappears into the building and returns with a yellow plastic bucket filled with a mixture of horse pellets, oats and chaff. He adjusts the mixture so there are less pellets in the second bucketful; the third one is all chaff. It takes about half an hour for Milly to satisfy her hunger. The man finishes stacking the fencing wire between bucketloads, then goes inside to help another customer.

'That was one hungry horse,' he says, when Banjo goes in to pay for the food.

Banjo nods. 'Can I buy the bucket, too?'

Half an hour later, they are several kilometres east of Harvest. There was mobile coverage in town and while Milly was having lunch, Banjo checked Google Maps. He estimates they should get to Hay, the next town on their planned route, sometime tomorrow morning.

He tried calling his parents, too – all three numbers – but when nobody answered, Banjo left a voice message on the landline, saying he and Milly are okay and he'll call again tonight if there's a signal.

He had better luck with Mai. She sounded excited to hear from him. 'Hey, that was such a great photo you sent yesterday! I'm going to put it on your crowdfunding site.'

'Is it up yet?' he asked.

'Yes. Me and Amber set it up yesterday. I'll send you the link.'

She did send the link, but Banjo hasn't looked at it yet. He doesn't know how much data he has left on his phone. He needs to keep enough for Google Maps, otherwise he will never find his way to Canberra.

Do I really want to go to Canberra? he asks himself for the umpteenth time. All that stuff he said to his mother yesterday was what Mai had told him – they were her words coming out of his mouth. Banjo isn't an Eco Warrior. Sure, he's worried about climate change – everyone is – but it's not his responsibility. He only agreed to do this so he could raise enough money to keep Milly. Now he isn't even sure he wants to do that. His mother and Nan both think she'd have a happier life at that riding school in Gippsland, where she'd have the company of other horses and get lots of attention.

And where there isn't a drought.

Banjo makes a sudden decision. Leaning forward over Milly's neck, he says into her ear, 'Guess what, Mills – we're going home.'

Since leaving Harvest, he hasn't been paying much attention to his surroundings. What's to look at, after all? The road here is fenced, but beyond the fences it's just the same barren wasteland he and Milly have been travelling through for what seems like days. But when he turns his horse around to start their long, homeward journey, Banjo sees something different.

'Awesome!' he mutters.

A huge bank of clouds fills the lower half of the sky. Banjo can't remember the last time he saw such an impressive sight. It's a thunderstorm! But then he notices they are the wrong colour for storm clouds – they are reddish-brown.

28

A million Tonnes of Topsoil

Milly sniffs the air. She nickers softly and pulls to one side. She wants to turn back around. She wants them to ride away from the weird-looking clouds, not towards them. But Banjo holds her steady. He sits motionless in the saddle, transfixed. He has never seen anything like it. The clouds look solid, like an enormous red-brown wall. A mountain range. Why are they that colour? Is it smoke?

A breath of wind lightly touches Banjo's face and now he can smell it – dust.

Banjo has heard of dust storms, but he has never seen one. He's seen *sand*storms in movies. They have them in places like the Sahara Desert. The stinging, wind-driven sand sends everyone running for cover. A dust storm probably isn't as bad, but it sure looks scary. It comes rolling across the plain towards him, swallowing everything in its path, filling the sky. Suddenly, the wind becomes stronger; it nearly blows Banjo's hat off. He tightens the chin strap and narrows his eyes against a flurry of airborne grit. A swirling red fog closes in around him and Milly.

Everything turns dim. It's like night is falling in the middle of the day. A car goes past with its lights on.

'You win,' Banjo says to Milly. He turns her back in the direction of Canberra. But only to put the dust-filled wind behind them. He'll find somewhere to shelter until the storm passes, then they'll turn around again and head for home, once and for all. His mind is made up.

Fifteen minutes down the road, they come to a gate and a letterbox. There's a name on the letterbox: *T & E Shelter*. Is that a coincidence or what! But when he dismounts to open the gate, Banjo sees the name on the letterbox is *Shelton*, not Shelter. Still, regardless of their name, they're farmers – they *will* give him and Milly shelter.

The driveway is long. One side is fenced and the other is ploughed farmland. Banjo can't see further than fifteen or twenty metres in any direction, beyond that everything is lost in the dust. Except the sun, which is a dull orange disk almost directly overhead. But looking up at it is a mistake – Banjo's hat blows off. He watches it spiral away in the wind, becoming less and less distinct until it's part of the red-brown nothingness. Goodbye hat. Hunched low over the saddle, he urges Milly on through the blinding, choking dust.

Banjo doesn't notice the buildings until he and Milly are right in among them, when all at once they are surrounded on three sides by dark, ghostly rectangles. The long, low shape with a pitched roof straight ahead must be the farm house. A barking dog comes running out of the fog and starts circling them. It's a dust-coloured terrier, you can hardly see it. Milly snorts a warning and it keeps its distance.

'Get back here, Teddy!' someone shouts.

Teddy the terrier doesn't go back, but at least he stops barking. A man materialises out of the red-brown gloom. There's a tea towel tied around the lower part of his face. He drags it clear of his mouth before he speaks. 'Can I help you?'

'We got caught in the dust storm,' says Banjo. 'Would it be okay for me and my horse to wait it out in one of your sheds?'

The farmer beckons. 'Follow me.'

He goes to one of the sheds and heaves open a big sliding door. Banjo dismounts and leads Milly inside. The farmer switches on the lights. Red dust now hangs thick in the air. The shed is full of farming machinery, but one corner is fitted out like a stable. There's a horse there already, a small chestnut mare with a white blaze on her forehead. A second stall is empty.

'You can put her in here,' the farmer indicates. 'I'll help you get her unloaded.'

Teddy has followed them into the shed. He starts sniffing at Banjo's duffel bag as soon as it's placed on the concrete floor. The farmer tells the dog to scram.

'Have you got food in there?' he asks Banjo.

'Yeah.'

'You'd better bring it over to the house then — there are mice out here.'

'It's okay,' Banjo tells him. 'I'll stay here with Milly till the storm's over.'

'It might go on for hours,' says the farmer. He checks the water in Milly's stall and gives her some hay. 'In any case, the boys will love to meet you.'

The boys are eight-year-old twins, named Oscar and Harrison. Banjo can't tell them apart. Their mother's name is Elly and her husband is Tim.

'Can you show us your horse, Banjo?' one of the twins asks once the introductions are over.

Elly is rolling up tea towels and pressing them into the gap under the front door to stop the dust getting in. 'Nobody is going anywhere until it's cleared up out there,' she says.

'Have you had lunch, Banjo?' asks Tim.

They all sit around the Sheltons' big kitchen table, making their own sandwiches with slices of crusty brown bread. Everyone helps themselves. There's sliced-up cold meat and leftover vegetables from a recent roast dinner, as well as salad-y things to go with it. Everything tastes fresh and lovely to Banjo. Mr Shelton — Tim — is in charge of the huge teapot.

'So, Banjo,' he says, filling their guest's chunky china cup for the third time (Banjo was very thirsty), 'what brings you all the way out here on your fine-looking horse?'

Banjo has been expecting a question like this ever

since he arrived. He is surprised they have waited so long to ask. But it has given him time to prepare an answer that's not totally true, but isn't a lie either. 'Don't worry, I'm not running away from home or anything,' he says, faking a big smile. 'It's the school holidays and I was going to see my grandparents.'

'Where do they live?'

Banjo tells them and Tim and Elly exchange a look that he is probably not supposed to see.

Elly asks, 'And your parents are okay with that?'

'Totally,' he says. 'I have to phone them every night and tell them where I am.'

'May I ask how old you are?'

'Fifteen.' Banjo sips his tea. He knows there are lots of other questions they'd like to ask, but are too polite. He asks a question of his own: 'Do you often get dust storms like this?'

'It's the worst one I can remember,' admits Elly.

Tim turns his head towards the kitchen window, where there's nothing to see but dust. 'It's quite something, isn't it?' he says. 'A million tonnes of topsoil on its way to the ocean.'

'Will it really go that far?' asks Oscar or Harrison – Banjo still can't tell who is who.

Their father ignores the question. 'And not just topsoil,' he adds, 'but seeds as well. The long-range weather forecast predicted a 20 per cent chance of rain this month, so I took a gamble and put in 250 hectares of wheat. But instead of drought-breaking rain, we get this record-breaking dust storm that blows it all away.'

Banjo fiddles with his cup. 'Do you think it's caused by climate change?' he asks.

The wheat farmer nods grimly. 'Absolutely.'

29

Role Models

The storm continues all afternoon. Banjo plays Minecraft with the twins in their living room. The lights are on because it's so dark outside. Teddy is curled up on his mat. He can't go outside because Tim taped the dog-door shut to keep the dust out. Just after five o'clock, Elly comes into the living room with a towel and a face washer.

'Banjo, would you like to have a shower?' she asks. It isn't really a question.

Banjo's face grows hot. Earlier, she gave him another towel to sit on so the couch wouldn't get dirty. He probably smells, too – like he did when he arrived at Mai's place.

'I guess I should go soon, Mrs Shelton.'

'You can't possibly go out in weather like this,' says the twins' mother, sounding like *his* mother now. 'You're staying the night. Do you have any clean clothes?'

'I've got a hoodie in my bag,' he tells her. He doesn't mention the clean undies.

Elly looks him up and down. 'Some of Doug's old clothes will fit you.'

The twins have told Banjo about their big brother. He's away at university studying to be a scientist. Elly takes Banjo to Doug's room and pulls open some drawers. They are full of clothes. 'Take whatever you fancy,' she offers. 'But have a shower before you try anything on.'

There's a bucket in the Sheltons' shower. This time Banjo knows what it's for. He washes quickly, standing over the bucket so the slighty-brown water can be used on their gardens. We should do this at home, he thinks. He'll suggest it to his parents.

'I hardly recognise you!' smiles Elly.

Banjo has come into the kitchen for a glass of water. He's wearing a black T-shirt and a slightly loose pair of jeans with the legs rolled up at the bottoms. 'They fit okay,' he says.

'What did you do with your own clothes?'

'I left them in the bedroom.' Someone had put Banjo's duffel bag on Doug's bed while Banjo was in the shower, so he assumed that's where he'd be sleeping.

'I meant to tell you to put them in the laundry,' says Elly, busily dicing carrots. 'Along with anything else you want washed. I'm going to put a load on later.'

When Banjo returns from the laundry, Elly suggests he give his parents a call. He tells her his mother won't be home yet and he'll call them later. 'What's the signal like here, Mrs Shelton?' he asks.

'Not good.' She uses her chopping knife to point at a landline phone docked in its wall-mounted charger. 'You can take that one down to your room when you're ready.'

Your room, not Doug's room. Everyone is so nice to him. Whenever he or Milly have needed something over the past few days, someone has been there to help them. Banjo has no doubt he could have ridden all the way to Canberra if he'd really wanted to.

'I should go and check on Milly,' he says.

'Tim already did.' Elly is running water into a shallow saucepan now, being careful not to waste any. 'He's fed her, too.'

Banjo wishes he hadn't half-lied to them about his reason for coming here. He doesn't deserve everyone's kindness.

'Is there a computer I could use?' he asks.

Elly leads him to a little nook off the end of the living room. What once was a storage cupboard has had its door removed to make a tiny study. Elly wakes the computer and taps in a passcode, bringing up Google.

'Dinner's in half an hour,' she says, leaving him to it.

Banjo can't remember the link, but it doesn't take him long to find the fundraiser page. The photo is eye-catching. There he is sitting proudly on Milly down in the riverbed behind Mai's house. What was the word she used? Intrepid. Yes, that's how he looks in his stockman's shirt and hat – if you ignore that he's wearing school shoes. Milly looks the part too, with all their gear loaded on her.

But Banjo frowns when he sees what's written below the photo. His frown deepens as he reads on. This isn't what Mai said she was going to write.

15 Y.O. Hero's Quest to Save Our Planet

Banjo Tully was always going to be a farmer. For three generations, his family has raised beef cattle on their 300 hectare property near Big River, in far western NSW. Banjo wants to continue the family tradition. But his future has become uncertain. As a result of the current drought – the worst in Australia's history – Banjo's parents were forced to sell all their cattle. And now they have to sell Banjo's beloved horse Milly too, because they can no longer afford to feed her.

The Tullys' farm might be the next to go.

Banjo knows you can't make it rain. He knows the climate is changing. The world is getting hotter. There are more bushfires, more floods and worse droughts than anyone can remember. The polar ice caps are melting and sea levels are rising.

And Banjo knows what's causing it. *We* are! By burning fossil fuels and destroying forests, humans are changing the climate.

On Thursday April 14, scientists, environmentalists and concerned business leaders from all over Australia are attending the Climate Emergency Summit at the University of Canberra. They will be discussing ways to save the planet for future generations.

The Prime Minister has been invited to attend, but he is yet to say if he will be there.

Banjo will be there. He hasn't been invited! No kids have been invited. But they are the ones who will be most affected by the decisions made at the Climate Emergency Summit. What will the world be like when today's kids become adults? What will it be like for their kids? That's why Banjo is going – to speak for the kids.

Banjo looks up from the screen. He has never really thought about having children of his own – that's too far in the future. But maybe he *should* start thinking about the future. Suddenly it seems irresponsible not to.

He goes on reading:

```
Banjo will be riding Milly all the way
from Big River to Canberra, roughly
800 kilometres. It's the holidays, so
he won't miss any school. But he needs
sponsorship. It doesn't matter how little
you can spare – every single dollar will
help.

If we raise $500, it will assist Banjo
to buy food, accommodation and essential
supplies for himself and Milly on their
long journey to Canberra.

If we raise a further $2,000, it will
assist Banjo and Milly to get back home.
(Bus fares for Banjo, horse-trailer hire
for Milly.)

Any extra money raised will go towards
buying food for Milly once she and Banjo
return home. Who knows, Banjo's parents
might not have to sell their farm or his
beloved horse after all!
```

Banjo reads it all the way through for a second time. He has to admit that Mai is excellent at persuasive writing. If he was a stranger reading this – someone who had never met the real Banjo Tully –

he'd think the guy she's writing about totally *is* some kind of hero.

But Banjo isn't a hero. He's just someone who, basically, ended up heading to Canberra because a series of random events sent him in that direction. But now he's going home again and everything Mai wrote about his so-called Hero's Quest is fake news.

'Awesome!' a voice says, so close that Banjo feels warm breath on his ear.

'You're famous!' says another, identical voice, warming his other ear.

Banjo turns his head one way, then the other. The twins are leaning over him, one on each side, staring at the screen. He wonders how long they have been there. Quickly, he closes the fundraiser page.

'Awww, I wasn't finished reading yet!' complains Oscar-or-Harrison.

'Why did you shut it down?' asks Harrison-or-Oscar.

'Because it's bad manners to read over people's shoulders,' Banjo says, sounding like a bossy big brother. He rises to his feet. 'Let's go and have another game of Minecraft.'

Of course, one of the twins mentions the fundraiser at dinner. 'Banjo's going to Canberra to meet the Prime Minister,' he tells their parents.

Everyone looks at Banjo. His mouth is full of roast beef and gravy. He chews slowly.

'Banjo's a hero!' says the other twin.

'He's going to stop climate change.'

'And you need money, too, don't you, Banjo? So you can keep Milly.'

'That's enough, boys,' says the twins' father. 'Let our guest eat his dinner in peace.'

But Banjo can see the curiosity on both parents' faces. He swallows and takes a sip of water. 'I'm not really a hero,' he confesses.

After the dishes have been done, they all cram into the little study to look at Banjo's fundraiser site. Tim and Elly are impressed. They tell Banjo how worried they are about climate change and how it might affect their own boys' future. They praise him for what he's doing. They say it's remarkable that someone his age is prepared to stand up for what he believes in.

Banjo hasn't told them that all of it was Mai's idea. Or that tomorrow he's turning back. He should have admitted it straight away, but he didn't want to disappoint the twins. They think he really *is* a hero. He doesn't have little brothers and it's kind of cool how they look up to him.

'You've got a hundred and sixteen dollars!' yelps one of them.

There's a window on the right-hand side of the screen that records donations made to the fund. At the top it says: $116.00 raised of $2,500.00 target. Below are the names of the sponsors and the amounts they have donated: Harper Gason $30; Darcy $10;

Romsey Tayeh $2; Lily and Imogen $4; The Spencer family $50; Olly, George, Leo and Max $20. Banjo can't believe it – people really are donating money to help him get to Canberra!

He feels like a fake. He'll have to give it all back.

Even as he's staring at the screen, a new sponsor appears above the other names:

Archie Lawson $10.

One of the twins pumps his fist in the air. 'A hundred and twenty-six dollars!'

'It's going viral!' crows his brother.

Tim leans close and places a big, friendly hand on Banjo's shoulder. 'It's really good what you're doing, Banjo. Thanks particularly on behalf of my boys. You're a fine role model for them.'

Elly says, 'Your parents must be so proud of you!'

Banjo phones them later. His mother answers and puts the phone on speaker, allowing a three-way conversation. He asks if they had the dust storm and his father says most of it passed to the east of the farm. Banjo tells them how he and Milly got caught in it and the Sheltons took them in. His mother asks if he's been eating properly and his father wants to know how he's carrying all his equipment. Neither of them mentions the fundraiser site – they must not have seen it. Banjo doesn't tell them about it. Nor does he tell them that he's decided to come home – that can be a surprise.

He goes to bed early. It's lovely to lie between

crisp, clean sheets instead of in a sleeping bag on the lumpy floor of a tent. As he drifts into sleep, Banjo sees himself in front of the computer with the Shelton family crowded around him. *Hero*, it says on the screen. *Fake, fake*, whisper the twins in his dream.

After breakfast the next morning, Banjo asks if he can use the computer again. There's only one more donation since last night: Ryker and Kiki $10. He's relieved there aren't more.

Mai has posted an update on the main page. It's another photo – the selfie he sent from his last campsite. Beneath it, she has written: *200 kilometres closer to Canberra, Banjo reports that the drought-ravaged 'Wheat Belt' of Southern NSW looks as barren as Mars.* He should have called her last night on the Sheltons' phone and told her he's no longer going to Canberra. But he's a coward – he'll do it by text. When he gets back to Harvest, where there's a signal, he'll send her a few lines letting her know that he's changed his mind and asking her to take the site down. She'll be disappointed.

Banjo isn't the hero she wanted him to be.

All the Sheltons come out onto the driveway to say goodbye. It's a clear, sunny morning, everything is coated in fine red dust. Harrison – Banjo can tell the twins apart now – holds Milly's reins and the big mare seems impatient to get moving. She nickers softly and shakes her mane as Oscar reaches up to stroke her. Banjo straps on his helmet. His shirt and jeans feel light and clean. The borrowed clothes he wore last night are neatly folded in his duffel bag. Doug has grown out of them, Elly said. She has made sandwiches for Banjo's lunch and packed them in with the clothes. Tim gave him an old jumper and some warm socks, saying it can get cold in Canberra. He also half-filled a big seed-bag with horse feed and helped Banjo find a place for it across the front of the saddle. Milly looks like a pack-horse from back in the goldrush days – there's barely room for Banjo! The twins made him a card, with a drawing of him sitting on Milly and Parliament House in the background. There's a message underneath: *Banjo + Milly, happy travells*.

The Sheltons stand waving as Banjo rides away. He feels lonely already. All he does these days is say goodbye to people. Nobody could blame him for going home.

The driveway is arrow-straight. They will be able to watch him and Milly all the way to the highway. But by the time they reach the gate and Banjo dismounts to open it, the family has gone inside. That's good, he thinks. They won't see him ride off in the wrong direction.

He latches the gate and mounts up again. How long will it take to go home? A car sweeps by, pulling a red train of dust behind it. Banjo sits motionless in the saddle, watching the dust slowly settle. The road surface has changed. Yesterday it was grey bitumen, today it's the colour of blown-away topsoil. If he looked hard enough, he might even see wheat seeds. Poor Mr Shelton. Banjo remembers how the twins' father placed a big hand on his shoulder last night and called him a role model.

How did he get into this whole, stupid situation?

It started as a lame protest about not getting a free movie pass because he lived too far from school to ride there on his bike. Then it was about his parents selling Milly. But Banjo's eyes have been opened since then – there are more important things than free movie passes or keeping your horse.

The future of the planet, for example.

Milly is becoming restless beneath him. She's ready to go. Banjo feels ready, too. He gives the left rein a little tweak and nudges her with his right knee.

'Let's be role models, Mills.'

30

In Good Hands

The famous Hay Plains are so flat that Banjo can see the town for half an hour before he and Milly finally get there. They stop at a little green park where there's a public toilet. As he stiffly dismounts, Banjo notices the grass needs mowing. Water restrictions must be different here, he thinks. Or perhaps they use bore water. Anyway, Milly can help out. Checking first to make sure nobody's around, he tethers her to a park bench with Jabba's useful rope, then fills her new yellow bucket with water from a tap behind the toilets.

Across the road from the park is a little grocery shop with a *Hot Pies* sign out the front. It's a bit early for lunch but he's hungry, so why not? They can stop again later and Banjo will eat Elly's sandwiches then. He buys a choc chip muffin too and six muesli bars to take with him, as well as a big bottle of lemonade to have with his pie. The lemonade is deliciously cold, but it's not as good as Mai's.

Hay is slightly bigger – and certainly much busier – than Harvest. The highway passes right through the centre of town. Banjo feels conspicuous riding a horse down the main street. The other road-users are courteous; they slow their vehicles and give Milly lots of room. People on the footpaths turn to stare. Banjo hopes Milly doesn't disgrace herself again like she did in the McDonald's drive-through the other day. If she does, he'll pretend not to notice and keep riding. Fortunately, that's not necessary; Milly waits until the town is well behind them before gifting some useful nutrients to the struggling roadside weeds.

Barely ten seconds later a white car overtakes them, slows and pulls over. The driver's door pops open and a woman climbs out. She's wearing a white top and dark trousers. Banjo's thoughts immediately loop back to Milly grazing in the park. Are we in trouble again? he wonders. But the woman's frizzy hair is dyed bright pink and you can't really be nervous of someone whose head looks like it's growing fairy floss. Anyway, she's smiling as she walks to meet them. She waves her phone in greeting. 'Hi there! You'll probably think I'm being nosy, but I was just wondering where you're going?'

Banjo reins Milly to stop. 'Canberra,' he says.

The fairy floss woman introduces herself as Loren Gourlay. She's the editor of the *Hay Gazette*. She saw Banjo riding his loaded-up horse past her office window in Lachlan Street twenty minutes ago and wondered if there was a story in it.

'Eco Warrior' Speaks for His Generation

Banjo Tully is not spending these school holidays hanging out with his friends like most boys his age. Instead, the fifteen-year-old Year Nine student from Big River is riding his horse to Canberra. Banjo passed through Hay this week and took time out from his 822-kilometre journey to speak to the Gazette.

'I'm going to the Climate Emergency Summit on Thursday 14 April,' he told the editor. 'I want to represent the generations who will be most affected by climate change if nothing is done to stop it.'

Banjo, whose family farm has been devastated by the ongoing drought, believes the Australian government is not doing enough to reduce the burning of fossil fuels that is contributing to global warming.

'I'll tell them to think about their kids,' he said.

When asked what his parents think about their own 'kid' riding all that way on a horse and camping out alone every night in the outback, Banjo said they know he can look after himself. But he phones them every day so they won't worry too much.

It is the Gazette's opinion that this country will be in good hands if young citizens like Banjo lead it into the future.

Readers can follow Banjo's extraordinary journey on his GoFundMe site. A link is provided on the Gazette's website.

31

Drought Aid

They run out of water the next day. Banjo thought they'd have enough to get to Narrandera, but it's been their hottest day so far and he and Milly have emptied their six bottles, which he topped up yesterday in Hay. He was going to refill them in Carrathool, the last place they passed through, but a sign at the abandoned railway station where they stopped warned that the tap water was recycled. Banjo should have filled the bottles anyway – Milly can drink recycled water – but he thought there'd be a park or a service station further on. When he realised there wasn't, he should have turned Milly around and ridden back into the village.

Now it's too late. They are halfway between Carrathool and Narrandera. The huge hot sun is blazing down pitilessly from the bleached-out autumn sky, shimmery waves of heat jiggle back and forth across the treadmill of bitumen that unrolls endlessly ahead of them and Banjo's mouth feels so dry he couldn't spit if he tried. Milly is suffering, too. It's worse for her, because not only is she walking,

walking, walking, but she's carrying Banjo and all his supplies. Their situation is becoming desperate. He will have to flag down a passing car and ask for water.

The first vehicle to stop is an old, rusty-orange VW van that needs a new muffler. A few days ago, Milly would have shied away from the rattly din it makes as it pulls over next to them, but she's used to traffic now. Banjo thanks them for stopping. It's a three-man band on their way to a country music festival in Broken Hill. They don't have any water at all – which shows Banjo they're country singers, not country people – but they offer him a can of beer. It's a funny story he will tell his parents when he phones them tonight . . . and they'll be pleased he didn't take it.

Next to stop is a family from Hay, going to visit their three children's grandparents in Wagga Wagga. They *are* country people and the father fills all six of Banjo's bottles from a plastic jerry can in the back of their loaded-up station wagon. He half-fills Milly's bucket as well. Before they drive off, Banjo asks if they read today's *Gazette*, but the mother says they left home before it was delivered.

After they've gone, he drinks nearly half the warmish water from one of the newly-filled bottles, then tips what's left into Milly's bucket. She's a slow drinker. While he waits for her to finish, Banjo digs out two of the four muesli bars left over from yesterday and slowly eats them. He's tempted to have another, but decides not to. The last of the horse food Tim Shelton gave them ran out this morning and it doesn't seem right to pig out while Milly goes hungry.

Finding food for her is an ongoing problem.

They come across Milly's next meal about fifteen minutes later. There are trees along this stretch of highway, so Banjo doesn't see what's ahead until Milly brings him slowly around a long, sweeping bend. A big, shiny green and white Kenworth, its two trailers loaded sky-high with what look like hay bales, has pulled over into the gravel on the far side of the road. About 100 metres behind it, a man, who must be its driver, is clearing a spillage of loose hay off the shimmering tarmac. A bale must have fallen off the back of his truck and broken apart on the road.

Bad luck for the truckie, thinks Banjo, good luck for Milly.

They clip-clop past the Kenworth and continue down the highway towards the distant figure. He has cleared most of the spilt hay off the road now and made an untidy, yellow pile halfway to the trees.

'G'day,' Banjo greets him. 'Is that hay or straw?'

'Hay.' The driver straightens up and wipes his forehead. He's a big man, with thick arms and sweat patches on his rumpled blue shirt. 'Hay bound for Hay, if you can believe it,' he says, shaking his head. 'But at the rate I'm going, not much will get there – this is the third bale I've lost today.'

'Is it all right if my horse eats it?'

'Help yourself.' The truckie walks around behind Milly; he seems interested in the way all Banjo's gear has been tied on. 'How are you at tying knots?' he asks.

While Milly eats her lunch, Banjo shows him how to make a trucker's hitch. It seems funny – he assumed every truckie would know that basic knot. While they work their way around the truck, retying all the ropes that have come loose, the Kenworth driver explains that he normally drives refrigeration trucks, where everything comes wrapped on pallets. Today's run is a volunteer job: he's delivering hay for a charity called Rural Aid. People all over Australia pay for haybales and donate them to Rural Aid, which distributes them at no cost to farmers affected by the drought.

Too late for my farm, Banjo thinks. All their cattle ran out of food about a year ago. At least Milly is benefitting from it. Whoever donated that broken bale probably wouldn't mind it being eaten by a drought-affected horse.

'So what's your story, mate?' the truckie asks, when they have finished tying down the remaining haybales. 'Where are you and your horse off to?'

Banjo gazes off down the next long, straight, boring section of highway that ends in a silvery reflection of the sky. 'Canberra.'

The truckie laughs. 'You're having me on!'

'I'm not.' Banjo slaps at a fly. 'Have you heard of the Climate Emergency Summit?'

When he has heard the full story, the truckie solemnly shakes Banjo's hand. 'Good on you, mate,' he says. 'I hope you save the world.'

32

What Are We Going to Do?

By the time they arrive in Narrandera, late in the following afternoon, Banjo and Milly are expected. A green Hyundai hatchback approaches from the town centre, flashing its lights. It performs a careful U-turn and a tall, shaven-headed man climbs out.

'Good afternoon,' he greets them. 'Are you Banjo Tully?'

His name is Luke Mullins and he writes for the *Narrandera Herald*. He found the article about Banjo in the online edition of the *Hay Gazette* and wants to write a feature story.

'Where are you stopping tonight?' he adds, shielding his eyes from the glare of the setting sun. 'My parents own a little hobby farm just down the road. They said to tell you you're welcome to stay with them tonight. They've even bought some food for your horse.'

Over the next few days, Banjo and Milly are front-page news in three other small country newspapers. People other than journalists are beginning to recognise them too. In the little village of Nangus, somewhere between Junee and Gundagai, a woman hurries out of the general store and hands Banjo a bottle of orange juice and a freshly-baked date scone.

A few kilometres further on, two excited, university-aged girls in a little red Mazda with P-plates stop to take selfies with the now famous 'Eco Warrior'.

On a lonely stretch of highway near Tumut, a smartly dressed, older couple in a silver-grey Porsche Panamera invite Banjo and Milly to stay overnight at their nearby horse stud.

The following morning, a journalist from ABC Riverina catches up with them on the winding road near Brindabella National Park. Banjo does his first radio interview in a white van parked next to a paddock full of curious sheep. He is becoming better at being a celebrity now and knows what the interviewers want to hear. They seem amazed that a fifteen-year-old can be so independent and resourceful that his parents will allow him to ride 822 kilometres alone on his horse. They also like hearing about all the people who have helped him and Milly along the way, by giving them food and water and sometimes a place to stay overnight.

Most of all, the interviewers want to know about the whole Eco Warrior thing. Banjo finds himself repeating a mix of what Mai wrote on his fundraiser site and what he heard on the car radio with his mother that day. The first couple of times, it felt phoney. But after everything he has seen, heard and thought about over the past week-and-a-bit (and there has been a lot of time to think), Banjo has become increasingly unsure which of those beliefs are other people's and which are his own.

Today, after all the usual questions, the ABC interviewer asks one he hasn't had before: 'And what arrangements have you made with the convenors of the Summit?'

Banjo feels his face turn red. He isn't sure what a convenor is, but he guesses it's a fancy word for the people organising the event. 'I . . . um . . . actually, my friend Mai Le is dealing with all that.'

Fortunately, it's not live-to-air. The interviewer, a gently spoken woman named Pilar, nods at the technician, who stops recording. 'Sorry about that, Banjo.' She has a soft-eyed smile that reminds him of Nan. 'We can edit that out later. Would it be all right if you gave me your friend's details, so I can give her a call this afternoon?'

As soon as the ABC van has driven off, Banjo tries phoning Mai to warn her, but as usual there's no mobile reception. They should have talked about this before. Ever since setting out for Canberra, he has worried about what will happen when he gets there. He hasn't brought the subject up with Mai in their frequent night-time conversations because, secretly, Banjo hopes *nothing* will happen. Simply by riding all the way to the Climate Emergency Summit, he's getting the message across: that the people with the power to change things should think about their kids. The word is spreading. In fact, it's spreading faster than seems possible. Last night when Banjo phoned Mai from the horse stud, she was so excited he had the pull the phone away from his ear.

'Banjo, what have you been *doing*? The site has gone ballistic! Guess how much you've got now?'

'I don't know.' Last time they spoke, two nights earlier, the donations to his fundraiser had just topped five hundred dollars. 'Eight hundred?' he guessed.

'Not even close!' Mai half-suppressed a little squeal. 'Banjo, you're not going to believe this – fourteen thousand dollars!'

She was right – he *didn't* believe it. 'Don't you mean fourteen hundred?'

'No. Fourteen *thousand*!'

Banjo still finds it hard to believe. Their target was only $2,500 – and there's nothing *only* about that amount! What's he going to do with all the extra money? Perhaps he could donate some to Rural Aid. Anyway, now his parents won't have to sell Milly. And they can send some of the money to the people at the horse-riding school to pay for the petrol they used driving all the way up from Gippsland and back.

Uh-oh! Milly seems to be limping. Banjo stops thinking about money and dismounts to see what's wrong. She's lost her right front shoe. He's been checking them almost every evening, but last night he forgot. And the irony is he was at a horse stud, they would have known a farrier. How long is it since she was last reshod? It must be two or three months, maybe longer. He's a bad horse owner.

At least there are no cracks in the hoof – the shoe came off cleanly. He can't see it behind them; she might have lost it a long way back. They have been keeping well off the road, so no passing vehicle will get a puncture if the nails are sticking up. Poor Milly, though. He leads her a short distance, checking her gait. It's just the slightest of limps, she might simply be favouring the foot because it feels different without a shoe. But he can't ride her like this, she might do some real damage. He checks his phone again. Nothing.

'What are we going to do, Mills?' he asks his big, beautiful horse.

They have to be in Canberra by tomorrow morning.

33

Treat Your Horse Better

The next town has a strange name: Wee Jasper. Banjo doesn't know how close it is, but he thinks it's quite small. They probably won't have a farrier. His best bet is to go back to the horse stud and ask them for help. But it's too far to walk. He'll have to leave Milly somewhere and hitch a ride. He leads her along the roadside looking for a safe place. There's scrubby forest on one side and rolling farmland on the other. Some of the paddocks are fuzzed with green. The drought doesn't seem as bad here as it is where Banjo comes from. If you lived in Canberra, it would hardly affect you at all. He sees more sheep in the distance. Where's a farmhouse?

Banjo doesn't find a farmhouse, but after fifteen minutes he and Milly come to a narrow side road signposted Cameron Lane. Six mismatched letterboxes stand in a higgledy-piggledy row at the corner. Through the fence, the land slopes down gently to a little, half-filled dam. It's the first time Banjo has seen water in a dam for years. If he can just find a gate, it would be a perfect place to leave Milly.

A little white van turns in off the Wee Jasper road and stops by the first letterbox. The window opens and the driver pokes a bundle of mail through the slot. He moves his van forward half a metre, then puts mail into the second letterbox. There's no mail for the third or fourth boxes, so he gets to drive a full metre-and-a-half before stopping again.

Banjo leaves Milly by the fence and walks over. 'Hi. I was wondering if you could give me a lift?'

The postman peers out at him. 'Well, I don't know. What about your horse?'

'She's lost a shoe.' Banjo slaps at a fly. 'I know it's probably out of your way, but would you be able to drive me to that horse stud a few kilometres back? I'm hoping they know a farrier who can come and help us.'

'That'd be Mick and Charmaine Spellman,' says the postman. 'They aren't home. I was there ten minutes ago and they were just heading off to a horse sale in Wagga. Where do you live, mate?'

Banjo tells him. He explains where he's going and why he has to be there tomorrow.

The postman thinks for a moment. 'You're in a bit of fix, aren't you? Tell you what – I'm nearly finished my run, then I'm driving back to Tumut. I think there's a farrier there. I'll give him a call and see if he can help you out.'

'Maybe I should come with you?' suggests Banjo.

'Better not.' The postman scratches his ear. 'We aren't supposed to carry passengers – it's an insurance thing. But don't worry, mate, I'll find someone to help. It might take a couple of hours though. Have you got food and water?'

Nobody comes. Banjo is still there four or five hours later. He was stupid to have gone along with the postman's plan. Why would a farrier agree to come all this way to help some kid he's never met? Banjo should have stuck to his own plan and got a ride with someone who *was* allowed to carry passengers, located a farrier and spoken to him face-to-face.

At least Milly is comfortable. Banjo found a gate about 200 metres along from the letterboxes. There's a chain and a padlock, but he lifted the gate off its hinges at the other end – an old farmers' trick – and let her loose in the paddock with the dam. She won't go far from the water. The way things are going, Banjo will probably camp in the paddock himself.

After everything he and Milly have been through, they aren't going to make it to Canberra on time.

A vehicle is coming. It's an old, grey Bedford truck like the one Pop used to own when Banjo's father was a boy, except it has a closed-in back instead of a tray. Banjo watches it turn in off the Wee Jasper road and stop near the letterboxes. A woman with a long, streaky grey ponytail climbs out and stretches. At first, Banjo thinks she's one of the six Cameron Lane residents checking their mail, but then she looks at him and asks: 'Are you the boy with lame horse?'

Banjo learns that the postman phoned half a dozen farriers before he found one who agreed to come to Banjo and Milly's rescue. Her name is Pam and she has driven all the way from Yass. She looks almost as old as Nan, but her arms are muscly and she obviously loves horses.

'What a beautiful big girl you are!' she says to Milly when they first meet. She raises an eyebrow at Banjo. 'Was she a show jumper?'

'Used to be.' He feels a rush of pride. 'My grandmother won a heap of medals on her.'

Pam examines the hoof that has lost its shoe, then she goes round and inspects Milly's three remaining shoes. 'They're all pretty worn. I suggest you get the other ones replaced as soon as you get home.'

Banjo nods. He doesn't tell her where home is.

The rear of Pam's truck is fitted out like a workshop. There's even an anvil bolted to the floor near the back. She measures a new shoe against Milly's hoof, then climbs into her truck, using an old wooden box as a step, puts on a set of earmuffs and bangs the shoe into shape with a big hammer.

When Milly's new shoe is fitted, Pam walks around her again. This time she runs her hands along Milly's back, across her flanks and down each of her legs. She even examines the mare's eyes, her teeth and her gums. Her mood seems different when she turns back to Banjo.

'This isn't a young horse, you know. She's much

too thin and she seems run down.'

'We've ridden a long way.' Banjo hates how his voice goes squeaky lately when he's feeling guilty or embarrassed. 'It's been hard.'

'Well, take my word for it,' the farrier says, rubbing it in, 'it's been a lot harder for her than it has for you.'

'I'm sorry.'

'Don't apologise to me; just treat your horse better in future.'

She returns to the cab of her truck and brings out an invoice book and a pen. She is no longer the friendly woman who arrived 30 minutes ago; it's just business now. 'I assume you won't be paying in cash?'

'I've got forty-five dollars.'

'That wouldn't even cover my petrol costs,' she says dismissively. 'What's your name and address?'

Banjo tells her and she begins writing it down. 'Where's Big River?'

'Out West.' He points in the direction the sun is heading. 'Between Mildura and Mungo National Park.'

The farrier stops writing. Her expression changes. 'Are you *that* boy?'

'I guess I am.' He shrugs.

She tears out the invoice and rips it in half. 'My contribution,' she says gruffly. 'Just take better care of your horse from now on, Banjo.'

34

His Own Words

A dark green Holden Jackaroo towing a horse trailer edges slowly past Banjo and Milly. It drives on for another 150 metres, pulls over to the side of the narrow mountain road and stops where there's room to pass. It's the same Jackaroo he saw five or six minutes ago, going in the other direction. There were two women inside and one of them waved. They must have driven on for a bit and found somewhere to turn around. Now, both women climb out and stand near the horse trailer, watching Banjo and Milly approach. One is middle-aged, the other is younger. He guesses they are mother and daughter.

The daughter speaks first, 'Banjo and Milly, right?'

Banjo, used to being recognised now, nods. 'Nice to meet you, but I'm kind of in a hurry.'

The mother smiles. 'We thought you might be. That's why we brought the trailer. Do you two want a ride down to Canberra?'

Ten minutes later, Milly is loaded safely in the trailer. Banjo sits in the Jackaroo's comfy back seat, sipping from the second of the two bottles of water the daughter gave him. Her name is Casey and her mother is Amelia. When Casey saw how quickly Banjo finished the first bottle, she said, 'Wow, you must be thirsty!' and gave him the second one. He explained how he'd let Milly drink all their water this morning because she was the one doing all the work. Grumpy Pam would have liked to hear that.

Casey talks to him through the gap between the two front seats. She's a bit of a motormouth. Already Banjo has learned that she and her mother live on the other side of Canberra, near a place called Queanbeyan, that they have two horses of their own and that they came looking for him because it might be scary for Milly on the busy city roads.

Banjo has been worried about that, too. He asks, 'How did you find me?'

'It said on your fundraiser site that you were near Brindabella National Park on Tuesday,' says Casey. 'Mum and I worked out you would probably be coming through this way because it's shorter. But we didn't think we'd have to drive so far to find you.'

He tells them about Milly losing her shoe yesterday and how they lost half a day's travel. 'It's really good of you and your mum to come looking for me,' he adds. 'I thought we were going to be late.'

Amelia, driving, laughs. 'It wouldn't do to keep the Prime Minister waiting.'

Hearing this, everything seems to close in around Banjo and his voice does that squeaky thing again.

'Is the Prime Minister going to be there?'

'Didn't you know?' asks Casey.

'I knew he'd been invited, but I didn't think he was coming.'

'It was on the news last night. Your "Save the planet for the kids" message has been getting so much publicity that he couldn't really ignore it any longer without losing votes in the next election.'

Banjo has no interest in politics. 'Is there going to be an election?'

'Not for a while,' says Amelia. 'But Casey's right – the Prime Minister might lose support if he doesn't meet you face to face after you've come all this way to deliver your message.'

'Who else will be there?' Banjo asks apprehensively.

Casey grins back at him. 'The whole world will be watching. You're going to be on live TV.'

The Prime Minister! Live TV! Suddenly, Banjo doesn't know if he can do this on his own. His duffel bag is on the seat beside him. Rummaging through it, he digs out his phone. But it's been ages since he last charged it and the battery is dead.

'There should be a signal here,' Casey says between the seats.

'That's not the problem.' He shows her the blank screen. 'Flat battery.'

'You can use my phone.'

Banjo remembers Mai's number from when he gave it to the ABC journalist on Tuesday morning.

She answers after six or seven rings, which is slow for her. 'Hello?'

'Hi, it's me, Banjo. I'm using someone else's –'

'Banjo!' she interrupts. She keeps talking, but it's hard to hear her because there are lots of voices in the background.

'I can't hear you properly. Who are all those people?'

'Sorry,' she says after a few moments. There's less background noise now. 'I just had to move a bit. Where are you?'

'Not far from Canberra.' He looks out the window but all he can see are trees. 'Do you know what's going to happen when we get there? Someone told me I'm supposed to meet the Prime Minister.'

'I know!' Mai laughs. 'Isn't that great!'

'But I don't even know where I'm supposed to go . . .'

Casey, who has been hearing all this, turns around again. 'It's at the university. Mum knows the way.'

'Who was that?' asks Mai.

'Some people are giving me and Milly a lift. They've got a horse trailer,' he explains. 'What happens when we get to the university?'

'It's all arranged,' Mai says. 'This really nice lady from the ABC called Pilar has been keeping me up to date. They've set up a kind of stage in front of the university. Someone's going to meet you and look after Milly.'

Banjo picks at a loose strand of wool. It was cold earlier this morning and he's wearing Tim Shelton's loose, old jumper. He'll have to take it off before he meets the Prime Minister. 'I'm a bit nervous, actually,' he admits.

'Don't worry, you'll be great!' Mai says confidently. 'I wrote a speech for you to read out, if you want. Will I send it to that phone?'

'Okay. Thanks.'

The phone pings shortly after they say goodbye. Banjo stares at the screen for a few seconds, then hands the phone back to Casey without opening the file. It was thoughtful of Mai to write a speech for him.

But when he speaks to the Prime Minister, Banjo will use his own words.

'My goodness!' Amelia gasps ten minutes later. 'So much traffic!'

They are somewhere in the city, heading towards the University of Canberra where the Climate Emergency Summit is to be held. The Jackaroo is inching along behind the cars in front. It would be quicker to ride Milly, thinks Banjo.

'There must be an accident,' says Casey, craning her neck to see what's ahead. 'They're making everyone turn off at the next roundabout.'

Sure enough, when they arrive at the big roundabout Banjo sees two police cars with flashing beacons blocking both through-lanes. A police officer stands in the middle of the road directing traffic around the wrong side of the roundabout. A second officer is sending them down the first exit on the right.

'This is ridiculous!' growls Amelia. Instead of going where she's directed, she pulls up beside the second police officer and buzzes her window down. 'We have to go straight ahead,' she says.

The officer gives her a stern look. 'I'm sorry, madam, the road's closed. There's a demonstration of some sort. You have to turn here.'

Now they are close enough to see what's happening on the other side of the roundabout. Hundreds of people are gathered along both footpaths. Some wave placards, others hold up pieces of paper with what look like drawings on them. Banjo finds it weird that so many children are in the crowd, considering it's a demonstration. He tries to make out one of their drawings.

It looks like someone on a horse.

Banjo buzzes his window down and smiles out at the police officer. 'G'day, officer. I think all these people are waiting for me.'

The police direct Amelia to the traffic-free side of the roundabout. There might be no traffic, but there are thousands of people. A hush descends on the crowd as Amelia and Casey lower the ramp at the back of the trailer and Banjo brings Milly out.

Suddenly, a child's voice breaks the silence. 'It's him! It's Banjo!'

A huge cheer travels back along the crowd like a Mexican wave of voices.

One of the police officers must have sent a message ahead on their radio. Two mounted officers come clopping down the avenue from the university end on glossy chestnut stallions. Milly nickers in greeting and one of the stallions nickers back.

'We're here to escort you to the stage,' its rider tells Banjo.

Everyone cheers again as he swings up into the saddle. The mounted officers form up, one on either side of him. Milly looks dusty next to the two brushed and combed police horses, but they haven't travelled 822 kilometres to get here. Banjo is so proud of her.

A chant goes up as the three horses and their riders make their way between the crowds that spill out onto the road from both footpaths, 'BAN-JO! BAN-JO! BAN-JO!'

Small children hold up drawings of him and Milly. Their older sisters and brothers hold up home-made signs and placards that say things like *Climate Action Now!* and *Ban Fossil Fuels!* and *Save the Planet for your Kids!* Mai would love this, thinks Banjo.

And then the strangest thing happens. No way! He can't believe his eyes. It must just be someone who *looks* like her. But the Mai-lookalike breaks free of the cheering, chanting crowd on Banjo's right and comes walking boldly out onto the road.

She grins up at him. 'Surprise!'

'Go back to the footpath please, Miss,' warns one of the mounted police officers.

'It's okay,' Banjo tells them. 'This is my Campaign Manager. Can we stop for minute?'

He swings down from Milly and captures Mai in a big, squeezy hug. Then he remembers that hundreds of people are watching and quickly lets go.

'What are *doing* here, Mai?' he says in a low voice. 'You didn't say anything on the phone.'

Her eyes sparkle. 'I wanted it to be a surprise.'

'You got your wish.' He can still hardly believe it. 'But how did you get here?'

'I came with your parents. Your mum phoned on Tuesday night and asked if I'd like to come and surprise you. Your mum is so cool! Your dad is, too. We drove down yesterday with the horse trailer so we can bring you both back afterwards.'

It takes a few seconds for her words to sink in. Banjo has been looking at Mai and ignoring everyone else. Suddenly he notices the two people standing behind her and it feels like he's in a dream.

'Mum! Dad!'

A TV crew has set up their equipment at the edge of the footpath, but this time Banjo doesn't care how many people are watching. He can't remember the last time both his parents hugged him at the same time. 'I missed you guys so much!'

'We missed you, too,' says his mother, kissing him.

His father squeezes him harder than Banjo squeezed Mai a few moments ago. 'We're so proud of you, son.'

'Excuse me, Mr Tully,' interrupts one of the police officers, speaking to Banjo, not his father. 'The Prime Minister is waiting for you.'

Banjo looks to where the officer is pointing. At the far end of the avenue, a stage has been set up on an incredibly green strip of grass in front of an imposing brick building. Photographers and television crews jostle for position around it. Up on the stage, five or six important-looking adults stand peering in Banjo's direction. He recognises the man in the middle.

'The PM can wait a few more minutes,' he tells the worried officer. 'I haven't seen my mum and dad for nearly two weeks.'

Drawing his parents to one side, Banjo leans close so only they can hear. 'Thanks for bringing the trailer. But would it be okay to take Milly to that horse riding farm down in Gippsland?'

His parents glance at each other, then back at him. 'Are you sure?' asks his father.

Banjo looks at Milly. He has only just decided. It's going to be hard, but it's the right thing to do – Milly will be happiest in Gippsland. He nods. 'Yes. I'll miss her like crazy, but it'd be nice for her to retire somewhere where there isn't a drought.'

Banjo gives Mai a little wave as he walks back towards his big, lovely horse and climbs up into the saddle for the very last time.

Then, raising his voice so everyone – all the children, all their parents, all the people watching him on TV – can hear, Banjo announces to Australia:

'It's time to talk to the Prime Minister about climate change.'